D0408065

# The Journal of Otto Peltonen

## A Finnish Immigrant



BY WILLIAM DURBIN



Scholastic Inc. New York

# Lehtimäki, Finland
## 1905

✣ ✣ ✣

## May 2, 1905

We are leaving for America tomorrow morning.

I'm anxious to see my father — he's been working in a state called Minnesota the past year and saving money to pay for our steamship passage. Yet I hate to say goodbye to Grandma and Grandpa Rantala and my friends.

In his letters Father has only talked about his job in the iron ore mines and how he is counting the days until we will be a family again. So when I try to picture America in my mind, everything is hazy. If it's like a photograph I once saw, there will be big white houses and broad, tree-lined streets.

Though I have never been further from my home than the Seinäjoki River, tomorrow I am headed for Duluth, Minnesota, by way of Denmark, England, and Canada.

✣ ✣ ✣

## May 3

I am writing this on the train to Hanko, Finland, the port where we will board our first ship. Sunlight and shadows flicker through the window of our rail car and make me squint. It is hard to write neatly with the constant rocking. My pencil point has broken twice. Luckily, I can sharpen it with my *puukko,* a fine knife that Grandpa Peltonen gave me the year before he died.

Keeping a journal was Grandma Rantala's idea. From the time she was a little girl, Grandma always dreamed of visiting America, and she asked me to write everything down for her. "That way, Otto," she said, "I can see it through your eyes."

It was one thing to imagine this trip, but quite another for it to begin. Even as I was helping Grandpa hitch the horse to the wagon this morning, it seemed like we would never really go.

The true fact of our leaving didn't hit me until we'd loaded our bundles on the wagon bed. Everything that Mother and my two sisters, Helena and Lisa, and I could take with us was tied up in four small sacks.

The only other thing we have room for is a wooden basket which Grandpa made specially for our trip. It has a hinged lid and a little iron latch and holds a few days' worth of food. I promised Mother I would carry it, and that is only right since I am fifteen, and in her words, "nearly a man."

I am nervous about the trip that lies ahead. What will happen if we miss our boat or lose our money, or if we get lost in a strange city?

As the train rocks back and forth, Mother is doing her best to hide her worry, but I can see it in her eyes. As usual, my eleven-year-old sister Helena can't control herself. For the last month, she has been complaining about how she will miss her school and her friends. Though she is quiet for a change now, tears are still running down her cheeks. I give her my handkerchief.

Helena did a shameful thing this morning. We'd just said good-bye to Grandma, when Helena leaped down from the wagon and grabbed her around the waist. She wanted to stay in Finland.

Mother started to climb down to get Helena, but I touched her shoulder and said, "Let me."

By then Grandma was crying as hard as Helena. Knowing we had a train to catch, I pried Helena's arms loose and pulled her toward the wagon.

She screamed, clutching at the sideboards and kicking her legs.

As I lifted Helena up into the wagon box, I caught a glimpse of Mother. I had never seen her look so sad. Mother is a pretty lady who was named after two goddesses (her full name is Minerva Juno Peltonen), but there is nothing delicate about her. Though she is going on forty and is barely five feet tall, Mother works with Father in the fields, and she chops wood and butchers chickens and helps birth the calves. I thought she could take anything, but Helena's crying had driven a needle straight into her heart.

I am thankful that my little sister Lisa, who is only nine, regards our trip as a great adventure. Lisa is quiet and thoughtful, and for the last hour she has been smiling at the green countryside blurring past our train windows. Without her courage it would be hard for me to pretend that I am brave.

## May 4

We are now at sea. The name of our boat — or should I say ship? — is the SS *Urania*. As third-class ticket holders, we are packed together like sheep in an undersized pen. The whole ship smells like rancid butter and coal smoke. Thankfully, our time on board will be short.

Helena's moods are getting worse.

## May 10
## Liverpool, England

We've been stuck at the terminal for hours, standing in one line and then another. Liverpool is a dirty city. The buildings are black from coal smoke, and the harbor is crowded with every kind of ship, from newly fitted naval vessels to old-fashioned wooden schooners.

Our food basket is empty. We used one of the American dollars that Father sent us to buy lunch. We only got an English shilling and two pence for change. I think we were cheated.

## May 11

We have finally boarded an ocean liner. Our tickets are steerage class — that's the cheapest passage available — and we are crammed into the lowest compartment of the ship. Though this ship is twice as big as our first one, the air is so bad that Mother fears for our health. Lisa and I are wretchedly ill. Before we left the dock a little boy threw up, and a half dozen others joined in. Now the smell of vomit mingles with the odors of sweat and engine oil and rotten bilge water.

The steady pounding of the engines vibrates through

the whole ship. I feel like I am trapped in the belly of a great steel beast and my stomach is knotted in pain.

However, most of the other passengers are young and carefree. One boy plays a harmonica and another a violin. People cluster around them and sing and dance long into the night. But beyond those laughing faces, the mothers with small children stand silent, their eyes clouded with a mixture of fear and hope.

## May 13

The cook had an accident as he was climbing down the ladder with our dinner. The ship lurched, and he spilled a big kettle of boiling soup on a Swedish woman and her baby. They both were screaming in pain, yet it took the ship's doctor, who was tending to a patient in first class, two hours to arrive.

## May 14

During the few minutes we are allowed on deck each day, the sailors point and stare. They laugh as we stand at the rail and gulp in air to steady ourselves.

The ocean rolls on. Is there an end to it? Will the streets of America be paved with gold like so many people claim? I have never heard so many languages or seen so many strange costumes as I have aboard ship. The clashing voices remind me of the Bible story about the Tower of Babel.

Sleep is hard to come by. The poor baby who was burned cries all night. If only someone could comfort her. My hammock bends me nearly in half, and last night the man above me puked right in my face.

## May 16

The baby died. Though Mother and the other women are doing their best to comfort the mother, she sobs uncontrollably.

The ship's chaplain buried her baby at sea.

## May 20

Lisa is full of questions now that we have reached the coast of Canada and entered the St. Lawrence River. She repeats the name of every town and ship we pass as if it's a magical word. Helena scorns Lisa for caring about the "dumb old boats."

In Quebec we will switch to a different ship before heading on to Duluth, Minnesota. I am looking forward to standing on a surface that isn't pitching and bucking in the wind. Mother says we'll probably stumble when we try walking on the ground again. For now I wouldn't care which direction I walked as long as it was away from Helena.

# Minnesota

✣ ✣ ✣

## May 21
## Duluth, Minnesota

We reached the Duluth harbor at noon today. They call this city "The Head of the Lakes" because it stands at the far end of Lake Superior, the westernmost of the Great Lakes.

Father was waving to us before the deck hands had even begun to tie the mooring lines. Though Father isn't tall, he has got broad shoulders and his skin is deeply tanned. Mother teases him about being a "black sheep," because he had the darkest hair of anyone in our village. I've got the same deep complexion as Father, but I've inherited Mother's straight blonde hair and blue eyes.

We shouted and waved back at Father, and he ran forward to greet us. There were tears in our eyes as he crushed us all in a big hug and remarked about how big we'd all grown.

Father's beard was wild and untrimmed. His eyes were bloodshot. His clothes and hands were stained a rusty color, and his fingernails were rimmed with red dirt. The stitching on his left boot had opened up to show the toe of his sock. Though Father was never one to stand straight, he looked more stoop-shouldered than I remembered.

As Father led us to our train, he explained that the red stains on his clothes were iron ore dust that wouldn't wash out.

When the train pulled up the hill and out of Duluth, I was amazed at how much the spruce swamps and balsam stands looked like our forests back home. The only difference was the lack of towns.

We asked Father about what sort of house he'd gotten us and how his job was going, but he wasn't very talkative. He apologized, saying that a friend of his had been killed in the mine last night. The man had slipped into an ore loading chute and got buried in the bottom of a train car. No one even noticed he was gone until they unloaded the car in Duluth and found his body buried under twenty tons of ore. Father said he was crushed so badly that they had to identify him from his brass miner's tag.

Father started to tell us about another accident when he noticed Mother was getting uneasy. "Sorry, Minnie," he said.

Lisa smiled and said, "Now you'll have us to talk about, Father." After that, our visiting turned to news of back home.

South of Hibbing we rode through a huge clear-cut. Back in Lehtimäki we log the old trees and leave the young ones to grow, but here they cut everything down.

The few pines still standing were magnificent, black-barked trees with high crowns of wispy green, but Father says they won't be around much longer. According to him, the Power-Simpson and Swan River logging companies are cutting every tree they can get their hands on. The biggest mill of all, the Virginia-Rainy Lake Lumber Company in Virginia, Minnesota, is sawing one million board feet of white pine every single day.

I asked Father why the stumps were waist-high in most places.

He explained that since the logging was done in the winter, the stumps showed how deep the snow got. When Lisa's eyes got big, he chuckled and told her that she would have to buy herself a good pair of snowshoes, or she'd sink right up to her ears.

## Later the same day
## Hibbing, Minnesota

We pulled into the train station late in the afternoon. Not only are the streets in Hibbing not paved with gold, but they are rutted with dusty wagon tracks. The town is a treeless place, and the buildings are crowded so tightly together that the eaves on some of the houses hang right over each other.

Father said new places are going up every day because of the mining boom. He claimed that Hibbing has grown from a handful of prospectors and trappers to over 7,000 people in just ten years.

Main Street was crowded with lumberjacks and miners weaving from one saloon to the next. Though the evening was warm, the lumberjacks wore wool shirts and pants. They smelled of horse sweat and whiskey, and their calk boots left nail prints on the wooden sidewalks. The pant legs of the miners were stained the same red as Father's clothes.

We only saw a handful of ladies. One of them was hanging her laundry out in the side yard of a saloon. Helena and Lisa gawked at the bright silk bloomers she was pinning on the line until Mother tugged at their hands and told them to look the other way.

Mother frowned at the stench of the fellows who walked by, and Lisa looked downright frightened. Both girls nearly jumped out of their skin when a Finnish man hollered at Father from across the street. "Fetched your little woman, eh, Uno?"

Father waved and said, "See you in the morning, Boom Boom."

Mother's mood brightened when we neared the end

of the street. She remarked that the homes were quite nice, but Father looked uneasy. He explained that these were all mining company houses and that he couldn't afford the rent.

"But where else could we live?" Mother asked.

Father waved toward a wagon trail. When a cluster of shacks came into view a short while later, he said, "Though it's just a squatter's camp and doesn't have an official name like the locations do, we call it Finn Town."

Up the hill was a bunch of small houses. The nearest place was sided with weathered slab wood that still had the bark on. The tar paper roof had curled up at the eaves, and it was patched in several places with tin can lids.

Mother took a quick step back as if she had stepped on something hot. Helena stared with her mouth wide open. My first thought was that if this was our new home in America, maybe Helena had been right for all her fussing and crying.

"Uno?" Mother said. Her voice sounded small and nervous.

When she said, "Uno," a second time, and Father refused to look up, she didn't need to say anything more.

Helena started to cry, and Lisa, who was tired from the long day, tugged on Mother's sleeve and asked, "What's the matter, Mother?"

Mother took a deep breath and said, "Nothing, dear. We're almost home."

## May 22

I woke up this morning with sunlight pouring through the cracks in the wall. A mosquito buzzed in my ear. I slapped and missed. Then I remembered . . .

This was America, and I was in my new house. House is too pretty a word for this place. It's a three-room shack with a second bedroom tacked on the rear. The extra bedroom is built out of pine boards which are so green that pitch is still oozing from the knots. The room smells like a fresh-cut Christmas tree.

I feel sorry for Mother. After I went to bed last night, she and Father talked in the kitchen for a long time. I couldn't make out all the words, but Mother's voice was high-pitched and trembly, while Father barely spoke at all.

Though Grandpa Rantala's house back in Finland wasn't huge, it was neat and clean, and the girls and I had separate bedrooms. Here Father has shoved a bunk bed and a cot into this little room and put all three of us together. After listening to Helena complain for the whole of our trip, I will now have to listen to her cry herself to sleep every night.

For breakfast we had stale bakery bread fried in lard and topped with sprinkles of sugar. Mother took one look at that poor excuse for bread and promised to bake us some *rieska,* a flat rye bread which is our family favorite.

As Father sipped his coffee, he apologized for the cracks in our bedroom. He said that the wood had shrunk more than he figured it would, but all we needed to do was tack some papers on the walls to make it snug and tight.

In the kitchen Father has hammered together a dining table and chairs out of some old shipping crates. You can read names like "Sears & Roebuck" on the boards, and you have to be careful of slivers when you sit down. The only other furnishings are a water barrel and wash basin next to the slop pail. Dupont dynamite boxes are nailed to the wall above the cook stove for cupboards.

The walls are covered with back issues of a newspaper called the *Mesaba Ore.* Most of the papers are turned sideways, and they are hard to read without getting a stiff neck. I learned some English last summer, when my mother's youngest sister — she married a British sailor and knows English really well — stayed with us while her husband was on a voyage to New Zealand. I talked with her a lot, and I even learned to read some English rhymes and stories. I asked Father why the newspaper spells *Mesaba* with an *a,* when we are living on the Mesabi

Range. He explained that Mesabi is an Ojibwa Indian word that means "sleeping giant," and it can be spelled three or four different ways.

Father has tacked copies of another newspaper called the *Päivälehti* on the wall, too. It was written in Finn, and Father said it gave the miners "the working man's news" and "the stories behind the stories."

Then without pausing for a breath, he told us how the mines were bleeding every penny out of the workers, and how they were firing anyone who even hinted at joining a labor union. Mother tried to shush Father to keep him from waking the girls, but he got even louder. He raged about big companies using big money to trample the rights of the workers, and he said that the miners on the Mesabi needed to stand up for themselves and "organize."

I was shocked at how Father sounded like an angry preacher. Back in Lehtimäki he talked politics with the neighbors, but the only subject that got him this mad was Finland's right to independence. His main interest had been his crops and livestock. Mother was looking at him like he was a stranger.

In the middle of Father's rant, a whistle went off across town. He checked his pocket watch and said he needed to hurry to the Helsinki, the mine where he works. Mother handed him his lunch pail, and he gave her a peck on the cheek. Then Father clapped me on the shoulder and said, "I still can't believe how tall you got, Otto. The fellows will be glad to know we got another man who can help us with the struggle."

What struggle can he mean? I thought. When I walked back into the kitchen, Mother had her face buried in her folded arms.

I did my best to comfort Mother, but even as I was telling her that everything would be fine, I was doubting it myself. Mother's normally got calm blue eyes, and her long, white-blond hair is neatly tied back. But today her eyes were red-rimmed from a night of crying, and her hair had fallen down over her forehead.

When Lisa called from her bed, Mother said, "Don't let her see me like this." She hurried over to the water pail and wet a rag to daub her eyes, while I went to the bedroom and read Lisa a story.

## Later

For the last year we've been talking about the wonderful life we would have in America. Since my father was the second-born son and had no hope of inheriting his father's farm, we worked as crofters — tenant farmers. We got tired of raising crops for the landowners and never seeing any profits. So we came here hoping to get a place of our own.

After all that dreaming, it's hard for me to accept the fact that I am living in a house with cracks in the walls big enough to stick my fingers through.

As soon as we finished breakfast, I explored the town. Helena whined to come along, but Mother told her to leave me be.

The shacks in Finn Town are built on a side hill so close to the mine pit that a sneeze could topple them right in. I can see why Father calls these people — I can't bring myself to say I'm one of them — squatters. Since no one owns the land, the shacks are set down every which way. Some are crowded within an arm's length of each other, while others are more spaced out. The wagon path through Finn Town is so crooked that Father says it was laid out by a blind man riding a drunken mule.

The shacks are roofed with everything from tar paper to birch bark and secondhand tin. Most are sided with slab wood, and the doors are made out of rough planks nailed together.

Cats and dogs and chickens wander all over. Nearly every house has a vegetable garden, but the only things growing this early in the season are rhubarb and onions. Father said there is a pasture up the road where a few people keep cows.

I could hear the chug of a steam engine and the creaking of gears coming from the open pit mine to the north. After reading Father's letters about working underground, I was surprised to see that so many of the mines were just big, open holes. This pit was at least two hundred feet wide. The red earth banks were eroded with deep channels, and a tangle of brush and saplings had slid down the bank. To the east a rail line ran up a more gradual slope. A hundred feet below stood a giant steam shovel mounted on a set of railroad rails. The back of the shovel was a tin-roofed building with a smoke stack sticking out the middle. Coal smoke billowed out as an enormous toothed bucket dug into the ore with grinding noise. Then with a trail of red dust spilling from its jaws, the shovel swung and dumped the ore into a rail car.

When the last car was filled, three men climbed down from the steam shovel, and the train pulled away. Then a whistle sounded and a big explosion went off directly below. The ground shook as a column of dust and smoke shot up in front of my face. I ducked my head, while the red dirt and pebbles rained down.

As I was brushing myself off, an old man waved from the doorway of a low-walled shack. He was wearing wool pants with suspenders and a long underwear shirt, unbuttoned at the top. He introduced himself as Arvid Makela, and he warned me that I shouldn't be looking down when a blast went off, because a little dirt in the eye was better than a cracked skull.

When I asked him how often rocks flew out of the pit, he pointed at a four-foot-square tin patch on his roof. He said a boulder had come right through and smashed his rocking chair to splinters. He said that the company thinks all us Finlanders are Socialists, and that they would love to blow us up.

With that, he wished me a good day.

## May 23

Today I walked the half mile into Hibbing. Along the way I saw signs for the Pool, Penobscot, and Helsinki mines. Half of the mines on the Mesabi are underground operations with wooden head frames built over the shafts, while the rest are open pits.

The ugliest thing about Hibbing is the lack of trees. Other than the gardens and rough patches of lawn, the city is a dull collection of telegraph poles and plain-looking buildings. The board fronts of the saloons remind me of stories I've heard about cowboys and the American West.

The streets and sidewalks are stained the same rusty color as Father's shoes. Ore dust paints everything from the wagon wheels to the rooftops.

Pine Street was crowded with horses and wagons. Along with the saloons, I saw a dozen general merchandise stores displaying dry goods, groceries, and boots. There were also several hardware stores, a newspaper office, a fire station, and some theaters. A new brick school called the Jefferson is just going up.

The fanciest home in town is a three-story place on a huge lot west of First Avenue. Neatly trimmed and painted, it has a pointed tower that makes it look like a castle. Two other big buildings are a store called the Itasca Mercantile, and the Hotel Hibbing, which wraps around a whole corner.

Once again I saw only a handful of ladies. Either there aren't a lot of women in town, or they don't like to go out alone. I can't blame them, since I half expected to see a gunfighter step out of one of the saloons and start shooting.

I saw forty or fifty saloons. There are separate ones for Slovenians, Italians, Irish, Finnish, and Cornish, yet I've only seen three churches so far.

## May 24

At breakfast I asked Father who owned the big castle-style house. He said that it belonged to Mr. Pentecost Mitchell, the General Superintendent of the Oliver Iron Mining Company. Father spit out those words like he was ready to give me a lecture, but he stopped short and wrapped his anger into one question instead: "United States Steel sure takes care of her own, don't she?"

## May 25

I'm feeling restless and tired at the same time.

It's hard getting used to all the noise in Finn Town. Every morning a wake-up whistle blows at 6:00, followed by a call-to-work whistle at ten minutes before 7:00.

If that's not enough noise, there are train whistles shrieking and heavy machinery clanging and dynamite blasts going off day and night. Some of the blasts rumble like far-off thunderstorms, but others are so close that they rattle our windows.

A forest fire is burning through the slashings east of the Buffalo-Susquehanna mine. Clouds of yellow smoke swirl through town. The fumes make Lisa cough and sneeze.

## May 26

Today I took Mother and the girls shopping. We went to a store that Father recommended, because the clerks know Finnish. With all the smoke and dirt, Mother has been worried about us getting sick. So along with our groceries she picked up a bottle of a patent medicine called Castoria.

The clerk convinced her that thirty-five cents for thirty-five doses was cheap if it saved a trip to the doctor.

I was suspicious from the moment I saw the label, which read "Promotes Digestion, Cheerfulness, and Rest." When we got home I asked Mother if she wanted help dosing the girls, and I volunteered to hold Helena down. But Mother had a different plan. She told me that the girls wouldn't even think of complaining if I set a good example and took a teaspoonful myself.

I was cornered. One spoonful convinced me that the taste of Castoria had to be worse than any disease it claimed to prevent. It was the oiliest, fishiest-smelling slime that had ever touched my tongue. But I did my best to choke it down and even smiled afterward.

After Mother dosed us all, she looked at the label again and asked me if I might need two spoonfuls since I was bigger than the girls. "No, thank you," I said, corking the bottle for her and setting it on the highest shelf I could reach.

## May 27

Walking from one mining location to another is like traveling to a different country. They call the communities around Hibbing locations because they are located right next to mines. The southern Europeans are the poorest — Father says they're even worse off than us Finns. You can tell their neighborhoods by the lively smells of garlic and sausage.

Father heard that people from thirty-five different countries are living in and around Hibbing. In addition to all the immigrant miners in town there are even a few Chinese folks who run a laundry, and some Jewish people who have their own killing rabbi to butcher meat.

## May 28

Sunday. Father sure is tuckered out after a week of ten-hour shifts at the mine. He's covered with so much ore dust that his eyes are two white holes. If he smiles — which isn't often these days — his teeth look twice their normal size. His clothes are stained the same iron color as his skin, and his shirt and pants are streaked with wax drippings from the candle that he wears on his mine helmet. During planting time back in Finland, Father could walk behind a plow from dawn until dark and never look half as worn out as he does now.

As tired as Father is after work, once he gets washed up, he's always willing to play a game with Lisa or read her a story book. Though Helena pretends she's too big for the stories, she listens right along. If there's enough daylight after supper, Father helps Mother with the garden. We are getting ready to plant lots of different vegetables, and Father wants to build a chicken coop.

Hardly a day goes by without Father talking about his plans for our homestead. "Then it will be '*Oma tupa, oma lupa,*' " he says. That's an old proverb which means "own house, own boss." As soon as we save up enough money to buy a horse and a wagon and a few tools, we can file a claim for our land. It would be easier to buy a cleared farm, but Father says that even a run-down place costs three or four hundred dollars. That may not sound like a lot, but when Father invited me to take a sauna last night, I learned why it's so hard for the miners to save up money.

I was surprised that Finn Town has a sauna. It's one of the biggest I've ever seen. Built out of cedar logs, it's at least twenty feet long, including the front half which is a change room. Father says he and the other fellows put it up last spring. On Saturdays the men take turns stoking up the stove and hauling water to get it ready. The women and small children go early in the evening, while the men take their saunas later on.

When Father and I arrived, four fellows were sitting on the cedar benches, soaking up the heat. Everyone kidded me about being a newcomer to the Range. Then after Father threw a dipper full of water on the hot rocks, they started talking about mining.

The men work in different mines, but they face the same problem — their wages are always changing. As contract miners, they are paid by the ton. If a man mines more ore, he should make more money. But I was surprised to hear that the captain of the mine can change the rate per ton any time he wants.

When the ore is coming out fast, the captain lowers the rate the miners are paid. So the fellows never get ahead. What's worse, the company deducts the cost of candles, blasting supplies, and tools from each paycheck. Though Father was supposed to get paid $2.50 per day last month, his check only came to $1.77 per day.

"We're crofters all over again," Father said, as he reached for the dipper. "We dig the earth, but the Rockefellers and the Carnegies are just like those fat noblemen back home who took our money without ever dirtying their hands."

## May 29

The temperatures are always extreme in Minnesota. It's shivering cold every morning until I fire up the cook stove for Mother, but it gets hot by the middle of the afternoon. Father says the gardens aren't safe from frost until June.

This morning Lisa and I were helping Mother chop a stump out of our garden plot. Miss Helena, who is too good to get her hands dirty, was inside in her nightgown when a mine whistle went off.

We looked up, wondering why it would blare between shifts. A moment later everyone in Finn Town was staring down the road.

"Where was it?" the lady next door called to Mother. When Mother just stood there, another lady across the road yelled that it was the Helsinki. That was all it took to set the whole population of Finn Town trotting toward the entrance of the mine.

Mother touched the shawl of a woman who was walking past our house and asked her what was happening. "There's been an accident," was all she said as she hurried after the others.

Mother stayed home to watch the girls while I lit out for the mine. I sprinted along the side of the road, skirting the crowd and praying that Father hadn't been hurt. When I got to the main gate of the Helsinki, two dozen people were already there, craning their necks to see past the engine house.

A group of men in front of the head frame were lifting two injured miners onto the bed of a wagon. The first man didn't look like he was hurt too badly, but the second man's leg was bent funny, and his pants were soaked with blood. I was shocked when I saw a splinter of bone sticking straight out below his knee.

I was relieved when I finally saw Father. He was waving at the wagon driver to hurry, and I hardly recognized him because his cap had fallen off.

Just as I was feeling good about Father being safe, the lady standing next to me moaned, "It's my Leo," and she fainted dead away. When I turned to help her, there was Helena, bare-footed and still in her nightgown. She was staring at the man in the wagon and crying huge tears without making a sound.

## May 30

Helena woke up screaming twice last night. I can't blame her because I couldn't close my eyes either without seeing the bloody leg of that poor miner.

## May 31

This afternoon I met a boy my age named Nikko. His real name is Kaarlo Nikkola, but everyone calls him Nikko. I bumped into him as he was coming out of Kleffman's candy store, and he dropped his sack of peppermint sticks onto the board sidewalk. When I said I was sorry, he replied in Finnish, telling me that it was his fault for not looking where he was going.

Then he handed me a peppermint stick and said, "You must be new in town. Why don't you come over and visit?" Before I could reply, he turned on his heel and told me to follow him.

Nikko is the liveliest fellow I've ever seen. He has fine, whitish blonde hair that hangs uncombed over his forehead, and his skin is so pale that little blue veins stand out at his temples. Though he's three or four inches shorter than me, he walks with such long strides that I have to hurry to keep up.

"My dad calls your kind Black Finns," he said, holding his forearm next to mine as we walked. I didn't know whether he was making fun of me or not until he laughed and said that no matter how much sun he got, he stayed as pale as a fish.

In the few minutes that it took us to reach his house, Nikko poured out his life story. He was hard to understand at first, because he switched back and forth between English and Finnish, but I learned that his family had moved here from Finland only three years ago, from Vaasa, a coastal city west of Lehtimäki.

When Nikko heard that I was from Lehtimäki, his

eyes got big and he said, "The home of the famous poltergeist?" I laughed and nodded. Everyone knew the story of our local ghost. This year a man had moved all the way to America to escape its haunting, yet the poltergeist had already shown up in his new house over here.

Nikko has a sister named Helmi who is the same age as Helena, and his father works at the same mine as Father, but his house is a hundred times nicer than ours. It's painted white and has a porch with two matching flower beds in front. I asked if his dad was a superintendent, but he laughed and said that he was just a miner.

When Nikko showed me his collection of books, I could understand why he was so pale. He must spend all of his waking hours reading. Though most of the Finnish families I know have a Bible and a handful of other books, Nikko owns five shelves full. He says he studies all the time because he wants to go to college and become an engineer some day.

He said I could borrow a book anytime I wanted.

## June 1

Tonight after supper I asked Father how Mr. Nikkola could afford such a nice house if he was working at the same mine as he was. Father got a funny look on his face, and he asked me to repeat the name "Nikkola."

When I did, he nodded his head and said, "Some of us get easy digging, and some of us don't."

Before I could ask him to explain, Lisa jumped into his arms with a book called *Tupa Tales.* Father smiled as Lisa snuggled down to hear her favorite story.

## June 3

Nikko came over and visited after lunch today. I was afraid that he might not like our house, but he said that some of his best friends live in the locations. After complimenting Mother on her housekeeping and smiling at Lisa, Nikko called Helena "a young woman" and invited her to visit his sister some time. Since I'd just called Helena "brat face," she will love him forever.

Nikko invited me to go fishing at Mahoning Pond. The walk along the railroad tracks was hot, but I had never caught so many fish so fast. We cleaned eighteen walleyes and toted the fillets back.

When Father got home and smelled the fresh-fried fish, he grinned. Slapping my back, he laughed and told me that I was worth my steamship passage after all.

Mother saved some of the fish to make *kalakeitto,* her special fish and potato soup. I can hardly wait.

## June 4

The latest issue of the *Mesaba Ore,* Father's favorite wall covering material, came out yesterday. Though my English is only good enough to understand parts of the paper, I can repeat the stories out loud to Mother and the girls. The front page articles were mainly about baseball and mine accidents. Right beside the news of the Hibbing baseball team beating Proctor 5 to 0, it listed three fellows named Leppi, Rasmussen, and Eckley who were hurt or killed in the mines this past week. I can't believe how the paper reports the deaths and injuries like they are giving the score of another game.

The other big news in the paper is that the local high school just graduated a class of six students. I wonder what school is like here in America? Father doesn't think I should even bother to go. He teases me and says they will send me to *kansakoulu* (that's where we send the youngest children in Finland), but Mother says any education will be a big help to me.

This evening Father took me to the community sauna again, and I met Will Leppi, the brother of the man who was killed in the mine the other day. Will is so discouraged that he is moving back to Finland. Father tried to convince him that conditions would be improving soon because the

Western Federation of Miners has promised to send union organizers to Hibbing, but he just shook his head and said, "That won't do much for my brother, will it?"

## June 5

Nikko visited again today. He told me about the famous Wright brothers who are working hard to perfect their airplane. They live in a state called Ohio, and according to Nikko, they can fly nearly an hour without stopping.

When Helena overheard his story, she interrupted. She asked enough questions to give him a headache. "Where is Ohio?" she asked. "How big is the airplane? Have they ever crashed?"

After Nikko went home, Helena kept talking about how exciting it was that these men with the flying machines were Americans.

I nodded, grateful that she had forgotten her self-pity for a change. Then she asked if we could go to Ohio and take a ride with one of the Wright brothers.

When I told her that the airplane was an experiment and ordinary people like us would probably never get to fly, her mood turned sour. She said America was a stupid place and that if we couldn't go on an airplane ride, we should have stayed in Finland.

I lost my temper and told her it was too bad that she couldn't fly away in an airplane and never come home. Helena cried for a long time after I said that.

Mother scolded me good, and it was only right of her. As the oldest, I should try to be more patient. Though Mother admitted that Helena was "impossible" at times, she made me promise to be nicer.

It may have been mean of me to talk to Helena that way, but one good thing has come of my outburst — she's been quiet for a change. I wonder how long that will last?

## June 6

Helena is back to her noisy old self already.

I met Mr. Nikkola today. He has an easygoing manner and best of all, he's always reaching in his pocket to toss Nikko a nickel or a dime for spending money.

## June 7

Though I didn't think it was possible, the mosquitoes have gotten worse. I patched the cracks in my bedroom walls, but they still manage to get in. As soon as I blow the lamp out and lie down to sleep, the pesky creatures are humming around my head.

One person who doesn't mind the mosquitoes is Helena. Though she complains about everything else, flying things fascinate her. Whether it's a hummingbird darting through the garden, or a hawk gliding high above the pit, she studies it intently. She even saved a bat that Mother found hanging behind the stove pipe this morning. Mother was going to swat it with her broom, but Helena insisted on letting it go.

Father said the mosquitoes and black flies will be ugly until the ditches and swamps dry up in midsummer. "And even then," he laughed, "the best they get around here is God-awful bad."

Mother hushed him for using the Lord's name in vain, but he only laughed and said that in Minnesota a man has to fight either bugs or blizzards.

## June 8

Father and I finished building a chicken coop tonight. I wonder where we are going to get the chickens? Lisa wants a pet rooster.

## June 9

I'm sick and tired of the dust. With the wagons going back and forth from Hibbing to Penobscot, Mahoning, and other locations, there is no escaping it. When Mother hung out her wash yesterday, a blast in the Sellers pit kicked up a big cloud of red grit. She had to wash her clothes all over again. That's no easy task either, since we have to pump our water from the well at the public sauna — that's a good two hundred yards away — and haul it by the bucketful. Then Mother heats it in a pot on the wood stove to fill her washtub.

The only thing worse than the dust on the Mesabi Range is the red, sloppy mud that comes when it rains. My boots and pant legs are already stained so badly that there is no getting them clean.

## June 10

The police arrested Arvid Makela, the neighbor I met on my first day in town, for having a "blind pig." When I asked Father why there would be a law against a man owning a pig with bad eyesight, he laughed his head off. I couldn't see what was so funny, until he explained that a blind pig was the same thing as an illegal saloon. He says lots of fellows buy a keg of beer and make extra money by putting the beer into bottles and reselling it.

Helena met Helmi Nikkola yesterday and she seems a little happier now that she has a friend.

## June 11

Lisa had a bad fall today. She and Helena were playing out behind our shack when she tripped and fell into an old test pit. (Those are holes prospectors dug when they were first looking for iron ore.) The side caved in and took her down with it. Helena ran home in a panic and got me. I leaned a pole into the pit and shinned down. It was lucky I got there fast, because Lisa was half choked with red dirt and buried from the waist down. Even after I boosted her up to Mother and Helena, she kept crying.

Helena surprised me with a big thank-you hug.

## June 12

Mrs. Nikkola invited Mother over to her house for coffee this morning. Helena came along to play with Helmi. Nikko and I grabbed some *pulla,* a sweet roll coated with cardamom and sugar, and were about to head outside, when the subject of the women's right to vote came up.

My mother doesn't care much for politics, but she's always favored women getting the right to vote. She believes in equal rights for men and women, though she thinks some ladies go way too far with their protests. When we were still in Finland, Mother got upset by an

English radical named Emmeline Pankhurst, who favored hunger strikes and smashing windows and bombings.

However, her attitude may have changed when Mrs. Nikkola showed her an article by former U.S. President Grover Cleveland. "Just look," Mrs. Nikkola said, pointing to an underlined section. Mr. Cleveland says "sensible and responsible women do not want to vote, and men hold political power because it is all a part of God's design."

Mother's lips got tight, and she said that maybe Miss Pankhurst had the right idea after all.

Mrs. Nikkola invited Mother to the next suffragette meeting.

## June 13

It's been raining off and on the last few days. I was glad to see the dust settling, until Father reminded me that all the water will help breed more mosquitoes.

Every patch of open ground has exploded with wildflowers. Lisa and I picked a bouquet for Mother and set it on the kitchen table.

## June 14

The police arrested a fellow named Sam Mastrianna for threatening the mine superintendent with two loaded revolvers. I figured he'd gone crazy, until Father explained that the company had promised Sam lifelong employment because he lost a foot. Then they went back on their word and fired him.

Father figures that the company decided that it's cheaper to stick with their standard accident payments, which are $300 for a death and $240 for a permanent disability, than to keep Sam around. Father said that United States Steel would go broke if they had to take care of every man they crippled.

Now that I know the whole story I think the police should have put that superintendent in jail instead of Sam.

## June 15

This evening Nikko told me about an old lumberjack cemetery on the east side of Hibbing beyond Superior Street. Before the town was founded, they buried the "jacks" and "gypos" in shallow graves, and Nikko claims that during the spring thaw a hand will sometimes stick right up out of the ground.

I never know when Nikko is stretching the truth, so I dared him to show me the place. It was getting dark by the time we got there, but I could see the outline of two dozen unmarked graves.

We walked up to the nearest sunken place, and I was shocked to see a stained leather boot lace tangled in the grass. "Do you believe me now?" Nikko said, bending down to give it a tug.

Afraid that he might just pull a boot and a bony leg out of the ground, I said that I believed him.

Later, when I was walking home alone to Finn Town, I kept thinking that every shadow was a lumberjack's ghost, angry at the boys who had disturbed his rest.

## June 17

Mother is working part time at Mrs. Lamppa's boarding-house. Mrs. Lamppa's husband was killed two years ago, and she has supported herself ever since by renting out rooms. Mother cleans on weekends and helps out with the laundry and baking. Mrs. Lamppa can fit only eight beds in her house, but she has sixteen boarders. They rotate day and night shifts in the mines and share the same beds. Mother says it's the busiest place she's ever seen.

Mother's wages are just two dollars a week, but she used her very first money to buy a dozen pullets. I can hardly wait until we get fresh eggs.

## June 19

Father has been talking a lot about the unfairness of the economic system. He says that all the laws in America favor the rich folks, and the rest of us are expected to live off their crumbs. I get tired of listening to him complain, but when I walk past Mr. Pentecost Mitchell's mansion and compare it to the shack that we live in, I can see his point.

I wonder how Mrs. Mitchell spends her weekends when Mother is working so hard at Lamppa's boardinghouse?

## June 21

When I'm not helping Mother with her chores, Nikko and I play baseball with some fellows on the north side of Hibbing. Though I can't afford a glove, Nikko says that I'm a good enough batter to try out for the local team, Brady's Colts. Too bad that Mr. Brady doesn't let Finns play on his team.

Lately I've been earning a dime or two by sawing up stove wood and splitting kindling for some of our neighbors. I think I can hit the ball so far because I've built up my batting muscles by chopping firewood.

## June 22

We got a hard rain today, and the streets look like small rivers. Lisa stepped off the sidewalk in front of the Itasca Mercantile and lost her shoe in the mud. She looked like she was going to cry, and I was proud of Helena for not teasing her. We all had a good laugh though, when Lisa tried stumping home with one shoe off and one shoe on.

Most of the open pit mines are flooded, but the Helsinki is still dry enough for Father to keep working.

## June 23

I used my firewood money to buy Mother an iron stew pot for her birthday. Lisa and Helena helped me tie a ribbon on the handle, and we made a card. Mother hugged all three of us at once.

It's strange that a small thing like a cooking pot could make her so happy.

## June 24

More rain. The last storm washed out the tracks at the Cyprus mine and flooded the Leetonia.

It was my turn to get homesick today. I'd just come home from Nikko's house — we'd been reading some of his books — when I saw a birch wreath in our window. Then I remembered it was the day of the midsummer festival, or Juhannus Day. To guarantee good fortune, everyone back in Lehtimäki decorates their houses with birch boughs. Girls even hang birch wreaths on the horns of the cows. Then at midnight everyone gathers around a bonfire by the lake, and we sing and laugh and dance until dawn.

Tonight as I get ready to put out my lamp, Finn Town feels cold and empty. I miss Grandma and Grandpa so much that I can hardly stand it. And when I look at Father's red-stained hands and hear the bitter edge in his voice, I think we've made an awful mistake trading our old life for this.

## June 25

As surprising as it may be, Helena's been helping around the house before Mother even asks. I think Helmi Nikkola is a good influence on her.

Nikko and I got a huge shock this afternoon. We were walking along the railroad tracks on our way back from fishing at Mahoning Pond, when a whistle blew to clear the rails. We stepped off to the side of the grade, and the track gang that was tamping ties just ahead of us picked up their tools and did the same.

But as the train got closer, I noticed one of the workers had stayed right in the middle of the tracks. He was staring straight at Nikko and me with a weird smile on his face. One of the men behind him opened his mouth to yell — I couldn't hear the words over the engine — and he ran forward to push him clear.

It was too late. By the time the engineer stopped the train, he'd dragged the fellow two hundred yards down the tracks. Nikko and I were shaking so bad that we ran straight home.

After supper Father told me that the fellow was John Kojala. No one has a clue why he would do such a thing. Father is writing a letter to his wife and five kids back in Finland. He will say it was an accident, of course, though we all know better. Phillips, the undertaker, told Father he'd never seen a body so busted up.

## July 1

I haven't felt like writing lately. I can't close my eyes without seeing the blank stare of John Kojala. Why would a man do a such a thing? As tired as Father is after a hard shift at the mine, I'm sure he would never give up like that.

Mother attended a suffragette meeting with Mrs. Nikkola tonight. She's excited about a rally and a march that the ladies are planning, to promote women's right to vote.

## July 4

To celebrate America's Independence Day, Hibbing sponsored a parade and lots of special events. Foot races were scheduled for miners, lumberjacks, fat men, fat ladies, and kids, but most of them were canceled due to rain.

Mother is interested in the Fourth of July. Unlike Father, she is trying to learn as much about the United States as she can. Though he understands English, Father refuses to speak the language because he says it sounds like "spitting and coughing."

On the other hand, Mother practices English all the time. When I'm talking to the two of them, I switch from English to Finn and back again without even realizing it.

Mother says we need to "Americanize" ourselves, and she plans to take her citizenship test as soon as the United States decides to let women vote. Father told her to not hold her breath waiting for that to happen. He scoffs at the Fourth of July and says the only independence he's interested in is getting free of the mine.

## July 9

Now that we've finished the chicken coop, Father has decided to build a small workshop behind the house where he can do woodworking. But Mother gets the first request — she wants real cupboards in her kitchen. I thought for sure she would ask for a nicer table and chairs before anything else, but she says those dynamite boxes make her nervous.

## July 10

The news from back home is getting scary. According to a letter from Grandma, though fewer Finn men are being drafted into the Russian army, the Czar has put a special tax on Finland. The Russian Congress — they call it the Duma — has been suspended, and the people who protested were gunned down.

Grandma says that Finland has called a general strike against the Czar. She fears that something bad might happen like it did last winter when soldiers with machine guns shot into a crowd in front of the Winter Palace in St.

Petersburg. They call that day Bloody Sunday, but as awful as it was, Grandma thinks that the worst is yet to come.

Father thinks that war may break out at any moment in the eastern provinces. As sad as that news is, it makes me feel better about our choice to come to America.

## July 16

Sunday afternoon. Father took us to a secret blueberry patch northwest of town. Lisa giggled when Father said that she had to promise on penalty of death to not reveal the location.

The berry bushes were thickest on a rock ridge between a logged-over area and a little stream. Mother brought along a picnic lunch and we sat in the sun a long time, visiting. For once Father didn't say a word about struggles or starting up a union. We picked six pails of berries and teased each other the whole way home because our hands and mouths were all stained blue from nibbling.

## July 17

A few motor cars have arrived in Hibbing. The spiffiest one is owned by Mr. Fred Smith. It's a shiny new, twenty-horsepower Haines-Aperson. We all turn our heads as it roars down Pine Street. Though the teamsters get upset and curse the machine when it spooks their horses, the rest of the town is envious. Helena would give anything for a ride.

With all the money Nikko's father has, I wouldn't be surprised if he bought himself a car. I'll bet that man spends more money on cigars than we do on groceries. When Nikko invites me over to his house for supper, we eat off real china plates, and not one of Mrs. Nikkola's cups has a chip! I can't understand why Father can't buy us nicer things when he works in the same mine as Mr. Nikkola, but whenever I bring up the subject Father ignores me.

## July 18

Father says they've hired a new foreman named Sam Carlson at the mine, and he's the worst one ever. According to Father, most of the bosses have been Cornish. He calls them "Cousin Jacks" because they come from a region in southern England called Cornwall where miners have been perfecting their techniques for hundreds of years. Father says they keep to themselves but are fair. They have old-fashioned expressions to describe the work in the mine, too. Father's favorite comes at the end of the shift, when they say it's time to "go to grass."

Carlson is a loud fellow who Father says is as dumb as a post and dangerous. He doesn't understand the need for safety and only cares about putting out more ore.

## July 27

Another thunderstorm hit town today. Though the Helsinki is open, Father says the lower drifts are really wet. It's strange that Nikko's father never complains about the water, while Father comes home soaked. Father and his partner are working on a level that is filled with springs. The other day he bought a bright yellow oil-treated jacket. Since he looked like a fisherman, I teased him, asking, "You catch any big ones?"

## August 5

When I am reading the *Mesaba Ore* out loud to the girls these days, Helena makes me skip the accidents. When we first moved to town she loved hearing all the gory details, but her attitude changed last week. We were walking past Art Heikkila's house on our way home from the store. The wagon from Barrett Livery and Undertaking was parked out front, and when the Heikkilas' door swung open, Helena gasped. There on a table lay the body of Art Heikkila. He'd been killed in a rock fall at the Utica mine the night before. Neither of us had heard about the accident, and since Art goes to our church, it was a big shock. It was especially hard on Helena, because Art had always called her "Helena of Troy" and teased her about being as pretty as the famous Queen Helen.

Helena stared at Art for a long time, but she didn't say a word until we got home. Then she started crying. Mother held her tight, while she kept repeating how cold and blue Art looked.

## August 10

We had another heavy downpour. Though all the open pit mines in the area have shut down, Father is still working. He sure is glad that he bought that raincoat.

## August 12

Things are so busy at Lamppa's boardinghouse that Helena and I have been going along with Mother on Saturdays to help out. I chop wood and carry water while Helena helps with the cleaning.

It would bother me to sleep in another fellow's sheets like these men do, but they are poor and single and have no choice. As the miners on the day shift are picking up their lunch pails, the men from the night shift are crawling into bed.

Our shack in Finn Town might not be too roomy, but at least I don't have to share my bed with a stranger.

## August 29

I saw an eclipse of the sun this morning. It felt strange to go from dawn to dark and back again in just minutes. I wonder how scientists can predict to the second when those things are going to happen? We can't even get a train to arrive on time in Hibbing.

## September 1

A farmer from Iowa named Chase came through Hibbing this week on his way to start up a farm in Bear River. I could tell that he was serious because he had a whole boxcar full of sheep and farm supplies, which he and his partner were going to haul north by wagon.

Father is worried that if we don't get a farm pretty soon, all the good land will be taken.

✣ ✣ ✣

## September 4

School started today. The principal placed me in the fifth grade, but she said I won't have to spend the whole year in that class if I learn fast. I wish I could take high school courses with Nikko, but my English isn't good enough yet. Nikko is still set on becoming an engineer, and I'm sure he'll make it.

I've been worried all summer that I might get a mean teacher, but I am lucky to have a very nice lady named Miss Adelaide Eaton.

## September 7

I have been promoted to the sixth grade!

Nikko says they moved him ahead during his first year in Hibbing, too, but he thinks that three days must be a record for the shortest time anyone ever spent in fifth grade.

My new teacher is Miss Hoefling.

## September 21

It has rained for nine days straight. Father says it usually dries out in the fall, but that has not been the case this year.

Thirty people in town have caught typhoid fever. I am sorry to say that Mother is convinced that our daily doses of Castoria are the only thing keeping us healthy.

## October 8

Sunday. The mine accidents continue. This past week Gus Almquist fell under a dinkey engine in the Leonard mine and got his head chopped off. Ed Day, a fellow Father used to work with, lost a leg in the Morris mine. Father and I went to visit Ed in the Rood Hospital. He kept staring at the ceiling and shaking his head. When Father tried to get him to talk, he only said it was a pity that he hadn't done things right and finished himself off.

## October 28

Firewood is getting harder to find. The local suppliers can't get any more hauled until the roads freeze up, so Father and I have been dragging in deadfalls from the woods.

We bring Father's old double-barrel shotgun along whenever we go out, and sometimes we come home with a partridge or a rabbit. Father and I are also scouting for deer signs, since the season starts next month. By the look of all the rubs and scrapes, there are lots of active bucks in the area.

## October 31

Annie Heikkila, the widow of the miner who was killed last summer in the Utica, has been asked to leave the Oliver company house she's been renting. Since Annie and her boys have nowhere else to go, she is moving to Ely to live with her sister's family.

## November 2

I have been promoted to seventh grade! Miss Hoefling said that my reading and my math skills were excellent, but she'd been waiting for my handwriting to improve. She finally decided that I have a "penmanship disability" and has sent me on to Miss Wilders.

## November 3

I can tell that Mother is lonesome now that the girls and I are at school all day. Though she's got plenty of work at home and the boarding house, and she goes to regular suffragette meetings with Mrs. Nikkola, I know she's missing Lehtimäki a lot.

Mother's homesickness started when Grandma wrote us a long letter about Mr. Vallinmäki, the organist at our old church in Kirkonkylä village. Mr. Vallinmäki supports the *Nuorisoseura* (a movement that tries to improve young people's lives), and he's sponsoring plays and poetry readings and outings for the youth. Helena's friends have also written and told her what a wonderful man he is.

Mother feels bad that we are missing out on such things. "All Hibbing has to offer is vaudeville shows and saloons," she says, with a click of her tongue.

## November 5

I turned sixteen yesterday. As a birthday present Father took me on an afternoon wagon ride to Sturgeon Lake with a friend of his named Riika Koskela. The clear water and pine hills reminded me of Lake Ähtärinjärvi where my grandpa and I used to go fishing.

Riika hauled a flat-bottomed boat in the back of his wagon, and after dark we rowed around a shallow bay spearing whitefish by lantern light. I had never seen fish so close to the surface, but Riika says that they come in shallow every fall. Whitefish are thin and silvery, and they swim with a wiggly motion. I missed every time until Father showed me how to lead them. Once I hit a few, we all took turns with the rowing and spearing.

We didn't get home until late, but we cleaned thirty-one fish in just a few minutes with Mother and Riika and the girls all helping. Then Mother surprised us by stoking up the stove and making a big middle-of-the-night fish fry.

After Riika said good night, Father gave me an even bigger surprise. He reached under his bed and pulled out a 30:30 Winchester rifle. Though most of the bluing was worn off and the stock had quite a few scratches, Father said that the rifling was clean, and it shot really straight.

"For me?" I asked, thinking the fishing trip was all the present I was going to get.

He grinned. "We've got to be ready for opening day."

## November 6

Miss Wilders has been helping me with my penmanship. She is patient when I dip my pen too deeply into the ink bottle and get dribbles and splotches on my papers that I can't blot away. I wish we could write with a pencil the way I do in my journal, but she says, "We must strive to master the more formal medium of ink."

When I asked her if I was improving, she said there is reason to hope that I will achieve "partial legibility."

## November 7

Father carved a toy train out of scrap pine for Lisa. He even attached little wooden wheels to each car and tied them together with loops of string.

## November 8

Helena has been visiting Helmi or some other girl from her third-grade class nearly every afternoon since school started. Her moody spells are fewer, but Mother is worried about her schoolwork. Helena's teacher sent home a note saying that she was socializing too much. So Mother has limited her to two nights of visiting a week. I hope she doesn't get crabby again.

## November 10

Deer season opened today. Father loves hunting so much that he's had the shotgun and rifle leaning in the corner for a week. Food is so expensive on the Range that wild game is about the only meat most people eat. The limit is two deer and one moose per license. Father says that will give us more than enough meat to can and smoke.

I sure hope we have some luck hunting, as Mother is low on groceries. Father's been working in hard rock at the mine, and his wages have been lower than expected. Lately my hunting trips have only brought in a few squirrels.

## November 12

Father and I both got our deer. His was an eight-pointer, and mine was a spike buck. We are hoping for one more.

The winter layoff at the mine could start any day, but Father is set to work for the Power-Simpson Lumber Company, just like he did last winter. They'll be cutting near Hibbing, so Father will be able to come home every weekend. Lots of the fellows are taking jobs in the logging camps further north, and they will not see their families until spring.

## November 30

We celebrated our first Thanksgiving in America today. Mother thinks it's important to start new family traditions, so she and the girls prepared a special meal of roast venison, partridge (Nikko and I got three the other day), potatoes, carrots, string beans, and wild rice (Mother traded some squash to an Ojibwa Indian lady). For dessert we had a blueberry pie that Helena made all by herself out of the berries Mother canned last summer.

Though the crust was a bit tough, Helena beamed when I told her that she'd done a fine job.

Mother wants us to have a meal like this every Thanksgiving from now on. You will hear no objection from me.

## December 10

We are lucky Father's got a job. Lots of the miners around Hibbing either can't or won't work during the winter lay-offs. Many of them drink and gamble away their families' money.

Mrs. Nikkola told Mother that Mr. Nikkola is pacing around the house like a caged beast.

## December 25

Mother and Father made sure we each got a Christmas gift. Father carved Helena a model of the Wright brothers' airplane out of basswood. I've never seen her so excited. Father is spending his evenings at the lumber camp, carving different sorts of wood.

Lisa got a spaniel puppy and was just as happy. Father kept the puppy a secret until he came home from work yesterday. When he bent down to hug Mother, the puppy poked its head out between his coat buttons and licked her arm.

Mother squealed and jumped back. She scolded Father and asked him how he planned to keep the dog out of her garden, but Father was grinning too much to care.

Father also carved Lisa another model of a toy train. This one is so fancy that the engine has spoked drive wheels, a smokestack, and a whistle; and all three flat cars are loaded with sawed-off sticks of alder brush that look like real logs.

I got a new pair of boots, which I really needed since I'm going through what Mother calls "a growth spurt." (She has threatened to tie a brick on my head so I don't grow right through the roof.)

We also received some surprise presents from Finland. Grandma and Grandpa sent me a new journal, and the girls got doll clothes. Mother helped me sew my new journal into the cover of the old one. Now I've got enough blank pages to last two or three years.

## December 27

It made me angry when I stopped by Nikko's house and saw all the presents. Though I know Christmas is about more than getting things, when I compare Nikko's brand-new Case knife to my old *puukko* and Helmi's fancy porcelain doll to the rag doll that Lisa drags around, it's just not fair. Why can't my father be like Mr. Nikkola, who knows how to fit into the American way of doing things?

## December 30

There was a long story in the *Mesaba Ore* about Mark Twain. Mr. Twain just had his seventieth birthday party in New York. He must be a very funny fellow, because he told all the guests that he owed his long life to the fact that he had "never taken any exercise except sleeping and resting" and had "never smoked more than one cigar at a time."

Nikko has loaned me one of Mr. Twain's books called *Tom Sawyer.* He promised it is a great adventure story which has some funny parts to boot.

## January 1, 1906

Mother decided that the only way we can save up enough to buy a homestead is to start a money jar. She says we'll need at least $200 for a down payment. Father cut a slit in a fruit jar lid, and then she screwed it on tight. Mother said no money was coming out of that jar until it was time to buy our land.

## January 4

Since Christmas Father has been working at the local Power-Simpson mill instead of their lumber camp. Now that he gets to stay with us on week nights, he is always lugging home scrap lumber for his carving. He's got a collection of special boards that have swirly knots and burls which he's saving for projects.

Mother asked him if intends to bring home a hunk of every tree that comes through the mill.

## January 8

Though the Helsinki is still closed, a few mines have started hiring back workers to get ready for the new shipping season. And one mine has already fired four Serbians who wanted to spend Christmas with their families. (The Serbians celebrate their holiday thirteen days after ours.) The foreman said it was their choice if they wanted to stay home. However, when they came back the next day, he told them that since they liked holidays so much he was giving them a special present called a full-time vacation.

"The companies will do as they please," Father said, "until we get a union."

## January 9

I've already finished *Tom Sawyer.* Though some of the southern style of talking was hard to understand, it is a fine story. I would like to read more by Mr. Twain.

## January 15

Winter didn't seem as long back in Lehtimäki. The girls huddle next to the wood stove, turning one side and then the other toward the heat, but they never get warm. It was so cold last night that my pillow froze to the wall!

They've cut back on Father's hours at the mill, and our money is getting tight. Mother has been out of flour for a week. All we've been eating is oatmeal and deer meat. I used to love venison, but I am getting so the smell of it gags me.

## January 17

Now that the mining is starting up again, there are already accidents. John Laurila — he's the husband of one of Mother's suffragette friends — fell into the timber shaft at the Shenango mine. The hundred-foot drop shattered his legs and hips so badly that there was nothing left of the lower half of his body. The funeral is tomorrow.

Every time the whistle goes off between shifts, I have to remind myself that Father is working at the lumber mill this winter.

## January 20

A boy in Hibbing named Willie McLeod has come up with a new way of getting around town. He strapped a harness on his dog and tied a rope to it. Then he got out his skis. When he gives a whistle, that dog takes off so fast that Willie's hat blows off.

The straight stretches are easy, but he's still working on the turns. Nikko and I were watching him yesterday when his dog cut too tight around the Blessed Sacrament Church. Willie hooked his ski tip on the flag pole and somersaulted into a snowbank. Nikko and I split our guts laughing.

Willie let Nikko and me both have a try, and we found that once that dog gets up a head of steam, he doesn't want to slow down. If Nikko hadn't dropped the rope, he would have been pulled right underneath a sleigh that was going past the livery stable.

I asked Father if he could make me a pair of skis, but

he's so busy making wooden toys that I doubt he'll have time.

## January 27

I'm getting more familiar with Finn Town every day. Just like back in Lehtimäki, I can already tell whose sleigh is coming by the pitch of the bells.

## February 1

The saw mill has Father working full time again. That should see us through until the Helsinki reopens. To celebrate, Mother bought a sack of flour and baked us a double batch of cardamom rolls.

## February 3

Mine accidents are happening almost every day. Sam Cokki, a bright-eyed young man who had just moved to Finn Town, got killed on his first day on the job. I felt especially bad because Sam had taken a sauna with us last weekend and told us about his plans to open a cabinetmaking shop. Like Father, he was only working in the mine to save up enough money to follow his dream.

Sam got caught in the chain of a steam shovel, and by the time they stopped the machine, his legs were totally ground off. Since he didn't know a word of English, my guess is he got hurt because he couldn't understand the shovel operator. Sam has a widow and three kids back in Finland.

Another Finn named Antti Kerkkonen was killed today when a chunk of loose ore split his skull.

Nikko and I went to Skerbeck's vaudeville show this evening. Father teased me about wasting ten cents of my firewood money, but it was worth it. They had a clown and a magician, along with the singers and dancers. The only thing I didn't like was a man who swallowed a flaming sword. It made me dizzy watching the blade slide all the way down his gullet.

## February 15

It was thirty-six below zero this morning. My boots squeaked so loud on the snow that it sounded like the soles were going to crack. The temperature has been below zero for twenty straight days. But when I complain to Father, he just laughs and says it was this cold for a month and a half last winter.

## February 20

The dynamiting is getting closer to town every day. Last night a blast in the Burt pit blew a boulder up into the street. The rock bounced twice before it tore down Isaac Haskenen's picket fence and ripped through the side of his house. Nikko and I peeked inside, and it looked like a bomb had gone off. Wood and glass and splintered furniture had flown every which way. Isaac says it's lucky the rock didn't hit the back of the house where his missus and kids were sleeping.

The mining company has agreed to patch up his house, but Isaac is threatening to sue. He wants to move somewhere else before another rock comes flying through the wall.

## February 24

Father has been called back to work at the Helsinki. The pay is better than the lumber company, but he's going to miss being around wood. Though most of the fellows at the mill complain about the sawdust and pitch, Father says there is nothing sweeter than the smell of fresh-cut cedar or pine.

## March 8

Now when the whistle goes off between shifts, we have to worry about Father again. Today Jaakko Koski — his son is in my grade in school — fell down the timber shaft of the Sellers mine and was killed instantly.

Along with the article about Koski, the paper ran a story about a Frenchman who has invented something called "motor boots." He's attached drive wheels to each of his boots and connected them by a cable to a quarter-horsepower motor that he has strapped around his waist. He can go twenty-five miles per hour down a fancy street called the Champs-Elysées.

## March 17

At school today I finally got a compliment on my penmanship. Miss Wilders said that I had moved beyond chicken scratching to "something vaguely resembling human script."

## March 24

Today Nikko's neighbor, Mr. Sellin, was thawing a frozen clump of dynamite in the mine, when all fifteen sticks blew at once. Everyone knew something bad had happened, because a blast sounds muffled when it's set in the rock like it should be, but this one was right out in the open like a giant firecracker.

The explosion blew off both Sellin's feet and threw his body forty feet in the air.

## March 31

We built kites out of paper and sticks today. Though the weather was chilly, the breeze was perfect for kite flying. I helped Lisa make her kite, but Helena insisted on working alone. Helena's kite looked like a fat butterfly with a too-long tail, and we all teased her until we found out that her kite flew twice as high as ours.

## April 9

Lisa caught a bad case of scarlet fever. Mother has been caring for her at home, but today she had to take her to the doctor.

✣ ✣ ✣

## April 11

The doctor seems to have helped Lisa, but she is still weak and feverish. Though we've been taking turns holding a cool rag on her forehead, she keeps moaning and saying that she's hot.

## April 21

An earthquake has leveled two-thirds of San Francisco. The paper says 400 million dollars' worth of property was damaged, and fires are burning everywhere. Hundreds of people are dead.

Though the blasting on the Mesabi is dangerous, at least we don't have to worry about the ground opening up under our feet.

## April 24

Lisa is finally better, but it took several trips to the doctor to get her cured.

Mother's money jar is empty.

## May 2

Miss Wilders took me aside and told me she was proud of how rapidly I've advanced this year. She promised that if I keep working hard I will soon be catching up to Nikko and the other students my age.

Though I'd never considered going beyond eighth grade — very few fellows do — she says that she will be "extremely disappointed" if I don't continue my studies into high school.

## May 3

Our venison and potatoes have run out, and we are living on oatmeal and fried bread. Money is short because Father has been working on hard rock and using more dynamite and fuses than usual. I can't wait until we get our garden planted again.

## May 6

In church this morning when Lisa held out her hand to get a nickel for the collection plate, Mother was ready to shake her head, but I slipped her a coin instead.

Though Mother hasn't said anything to the girls, she told me that Lisa's doctoring cost a lot more than she figured it would. I wish I could help out with the payments, but no one needs much firewood this time of year.

## May 19

The Western Federation of Miners union called their first meeting in Hibbing this week. Mother asked Father not to go, because she's heard that the company will fire anyone who joins the union, but Father said that if Western Federation President John Williams was traveling all the way from Denver to help the miners, the least he could do was walk down the street to "have a listen."

Only 32 of the 10,000 miners on the Range showed up for the meeting. Most of them probably have the same fear that Mother does.

## May 28

A rainstorm washed away most of our newly planted garden. Last night I heard Mother and Father whispering about their money troubles. Though they can pay for our daily living, they haven't been able to save a penny for our homestead since Lisa's sickness.

Today Father laughed when he read in the paper that the Wright brothers were getting a patent on their airplane. He called it "pure foolishness." Helena still insists that the airplane will change the world.

## May 29

After talking it over with Mother and Father, I've decided to apply for a job at the Helsinki mine. Though I'd like to continue my schooling, I know this is the only way we can ever save up enough money to get a farm.

## May 30

Czar Nicholas II has given women the right to vote. Though Mother doesn't often praise the Czar, she admires him for granting universal suffrage. Mother is thinking of writing a letter to President Roosevelt and telling him it's about time this country catches up with the Russians.

## June 3

The champion heavyweight boxer, John L. Sullivan, has been in town for the last three days. Though I couldn't afford to go to Sullivan's exhibition, I saw him in front of the Hibbing Hotel this afternoon. We have lots of tough lumberjacks and miners in this town, but there isn't a man who could last a minute in the ring with Sullivan. His polite voice, fancy clothes, and neatly combed mustache give him a gentlemanly appearance, but his huge chest and fists tell a different story.

## June 8

I went to work at the Helsinki this morning. Though Mother was crying as she handed me my lunch pail, she knows that it's the only way we'll ever get ahead.

After walking past the head frame of the mine for all those months, it felt strange to walk through the gate for the first time. The captain assigned me to the timber yard. Father said they would put me right to work, and he wasn't kidding. The foreman of the yard is a crotchety old fellow named Ole Swenson. His nickname is "Boom Boom," and he is the very same fellow who waved to Father our first afternoon in Hibbing. Without so much as a "good morning" or "how do you do" Swenson handed me a bow saw and pointed toward a pile of marked timbers. I spent the whole day cutting logs for support posts and ceiling planking.

Swenson is a surly fellow who always looks mad. His right hand is crippled, so the only real work he can do is drive a wagon. The other thing he does well is give orders.

The problem is his cheek is always stuffed with a big chaw of tobacco, and he is impossible to understand. Nothing makes him madder than having to repeat himself. Even if I say, "Excuse me, sir," he blows up like I just insulted his mother — or worse, accused him of being a Norwegian. (Father warned me to never say "Norwegian" within earshot of Swenson.)

When I got home, I told Father that I'd rather be working underground than taking orders from that grumpy old Swede, but he told me to enjoy the fresh air and sunshine while I could.

I asked Father again how Swenson got the nickname "Boom Boom," but he changed the subject without giving me an answer.

## June 9

I could barely crawl out of bed this morning. Bending my back for ten hours straight and ripping on that saw is the hardest work I've ever done. I even look forward to unloading the wagons, because it lets me straighten up for a change.

✣ ✣ ✣

## June 11

This summer Nikko is working as a clerk in Mr. Kleffman's candy store. I tease Nikko about having an easy job, but the truth is I envy him for having a clear plan. He's still set on becoming an engineer, and he knows he can't keep up with his studies if he takes on anything more than a part-time job.

## June 12

We haven't gotten a speck of rain since that storm last month. Mother says that if a forest fire starts, the shacks in Finn Town could all go up in a puff of smoke.

During a dry summer a few years back, three Range towns, Merritt, Mountain Iron, and Virginia, burned right to the ground.

## June 13

Though I'm finally beginning to understand Swenson's mumbled directions, I feel like I've got a permanent crook in my back. At quitting time I have to walk a ways before I can begin to straighten up.

Since I'm complaining, I will also add these to my list: blisters, pine pitch, black flies, and bark beetles.

## June 14

I've never seen Mother so mad. We got a letter from Grandma Rantala saying that Finland has not only given women the right to vote, but they have also elected nineteen ladies to serve in their new parliament.

Mother wrote a three-page letter to President Roosevelt. Though Father told her she was just wasting stamps, she ignored him. I helped her spell the big words. Mother started in by telling Mr. Roosevelt it was time America caught up with countries like Finland that recognized the worth of women, and she never slowed down until the bottom of the last page.

Whether President Roosevelt reads her letter or not, I am proud of Mother for speaking her mind.

## June 15

Father finally told me the story of how Swenson got nicknamed "Boom Boom." Mother and the girls were at a meeting with Mrs. Nikkola, and I was helping him repair the fencing on the chicken coop. As we were stapling some wire in place, Father asked me how I was getting along with Swenson. When I complained about what a grouch he was, Father told me that Swenson had had a very hard life.

I must have looked doubtful because Father went on to explain that Swenson helped him get his first job in Hibbing. It was at the Penobscot mine. But the Penobscot was so wet that when he and Swenson got a chance to work at a new mine called the Wheeling, they both jumped at it. Swenson's son, Bill, hired on, too.

"That turned out to be a terrible mistake," Father said, setting down his hammer and staples. Though the ore was rich in Wheeling, the foremen drove the miners like they were animals. The worst was a man named Angus McCready. He never gave a thought to safety, and when accidents did happen, he never even filed a report. Father said that McCready liked to hire bachelors because if one of them died in an accident, no one asked questions. Whenever a bachelor got killed, McCready ordered the men on the night shift to haul the body out to the rock dump and bury it just deep enough to hide it from the ravens.

Father's voice softened as he finished his story. Father and Swenson and Bill were fixing to go to work at the Helsinki. They had a week left at the Wheeling, or the Graves, as the men had begun to call it because so many men were getting killed.

On Tuesday Bill's crew blasted just before quitting time. It sounded like some of the charges didn't go off. But instead of letting the site stand empty like you should if you suspect a dud might be smoldering, McCready ordered Bill to go down and check.

Father paused a long time before he finished his story. Finally he said, "When we dug Bill out there wasn't much left of him."

Father went on to tell how Swenson went silent for a long time after. No one realized how deep his anger was until three months passed. It was a Saturday night, and McCready had been out drinking. Someone snuck into McCready's house, gagged him, and tied him to his bed. Then they stuck three sticks of dynamite under his pillow and lit the fuse.

Since McCready was such a hated man, the police didn't try very hard to catch the fellow who'd killed him. Though Father said that he and Swenson and the other fellows who worked at the Wheeling mine were questioned, no one was ever arrested. Swenson never admitted that he did it, but he never denied it either. "Shortly after the investigation was closed, the fellows started calling him 'Boom Boom,'" Father said, "and he's never once objected."

## June 16

Nikko stopped by to visit this evening. He lent me a copy of a new book called *White Fang* by Jack London. It makes you feel like you are right in the middle of the Alaskan gold rush. Nikko's got another one by London called *Sea Wolf* that I can borrow, too.

## June 23

The dry weather continues. Though the gardens are suffering, the local building projects are going great guns. Lots which cost $200 a few years back are now selling for $2000. The new high school will be ready in September.

Hibbing graduated four students this year. Nikko will be a member of the class of 1908. Though I don't begrudge him his opportunity, I'm angry that my schooling got cut short. Sometimes I feel like everything that I care about has been taken from me. First I lost my home and my friends and my grandparents, then a chance for an education. The question is what can be next?

## July 1

I got my first paycheck today. Now I know how Father feels. After all the blisters and bug bites that I suffered in the timber yard, I cleared just enough to pay Mother and Father back for the work boots they bought me last month. (When the shoemaker found out my Christmas boots were already two sizes too small, he was kind enough to sell us a pair on credit.)

Since these new boots already feel tight, I think my "growth spurt" must be continuing.

My paycheck would have been bigger, but the company charged me for two bow saw frames and one axe handle that I broke. It didn't seem fair for them to dock my pay for breaking saws that had already been patched together with baling wire, but I knew there was no use in arguing with that Swenson.

## July 2

Today I went underground for the first time. I've been promoted to the timber tramming crew, and I'm working with a young fellow named Wally Niska, who's been at the Helsinki for a year.

I will never forget how it felt to be lowered down the mine shaft. When Wally and I stepped into the metal cage, the first thing I noticed was a cold, damp smell. The cage was open on one side and the floor felt shaky, like a tree house swaying in the wind. A heavy metal compartment called the skip hangs directly beneath the cage. That's what they use to lift the ore to the surface.

A bell clanged, and the cable jerked as the steam hoist

revved up a notch over in the engine room. Then we fell. The cable reeled out with a rusty screeching, and the cage clattered down so fast that my hair blew back. Wally laughed as I leaned away from the open door and stared at the shaft wall and the upper drifts flashing by only inches away. (The drifts are the side tunnels that go out from the main shaft and lead to the ore pockets.)

When the cage stopped, I pitched forward and Wally laughed again. The bottom drift is called the Jenny Lou. Wally says the main drifts — the Sarah, Alice, Clementine, Susan, and Jenny Lou — are all named after the wives or daughters of the fellows who own the mine.

Wally struck a match and lit the candles that were attached to our helmets with wire holders and explained that our job was to deliver timbers with a four-wheeled cart that rides on the same rails as the ore cars. Though the miners have mules to pull the ore cars, we push our cart by hand, hauling support posts from the timber shaft to the end of the drift so the crews can brace up the walls and ceilings. Father says that timbering is critical in the soft ores of the Mesabi. He calls it "heavy mining," meaning that the loose soil is forever settling down.

I thought it was noisy in the timber yard with the sawing and the coming and going of the lumber wagons and ore trains, but that place is as quiet as a church compared to being underground. Hammers pound steel drills. Ore cars clatter down the rails. Mules clomp away in the darkness. And in the background the cable hoist hums all day long as the skip lifts ore to the surface.

With all the racket it's no wonder that Father is getting hard of hearing these days.

## July 3

I'm worn out by the end of my shift. I am grateful to Helena and Lisa who are helping Mother while I am at work. They are even splitting the kindling and hauling the water.

Wally is a nice enough fellow to work with, but he stinks of whiskey and chewing tobacco. He spends all his evenings in the Finnish saloons, and he's proud of it. He bragged that he went to a saloon last Saturday night and stayed there until shift change on Monday morning.

Though Wally is a smart fellow, I don't think he's going to have a brain left if he keeps sopping up so much liquor.

## July 4

Hibbing sponsored a Fourth of July picnic in the park today. A band played, and there were races for children with prizes in every age group. Helena won her race. She's too stubborn to let anyone beat her. At the end of the day a committee of mine officials gave awards to the best gardens in town.

It's strange being at a picnic now that I'm a working man. I feel like running and playing with the kids, but at the same time I know I should be acting more like a grownup. If being an adult means standing around and talking about the weather and drinking beer, I don't think I ever want to be a part of that group.

## July 5

I'll never get used to the smell underground. It's a heavy, musty odor, like a cold cellar that's been closed up for years. No matter how deeply I breathe, I feel like I'm short of oxygen.

Dust hangs in the air for hours after every blast. They set off the charges before lunch or at quitting time so the drift can clear out before the miners have to go back to drilling, but the acrid, burnt smell of powder lingers all day. I get lightheaded from the fumes, and sometimes the air is so stale that my candle snuffs out.

Wally and I eat more dust than the miners because we have to hustle our timbers to the work sites when no one's hauling ore. We do as much as we can during the lunch breaks and shift changes, but we go into the drifts sooner than we should after the blasts. Even with a handkerchief tied across my mouth, I get clumps of red grit between my teeth.

## July 6

This morning Wally and I got a late start from the timber yard. We got stuck behind Father and Mr. Nikkola and the rest of the day shift crew who were heading toward the main shaft.

As the fellows approached the head frame of the mine, I was surprised to see them drop a coin into a snuff box that was sitting on a stool beside the foreman. Every single fellow did it, except Father and a few other Finnish fellows who walked past the foreman without even turning their heads. Mr. Nikkola hung back until he thought no one was looking, then he set down a coin, too.

After Wally and I got to the timber shaft — that's a separate entrance to the mine where we lower our timbering down without slowing down the mining — I asked him about that snuff box. "It's a bribe," Wally said. "You give the foreman a tip, and he puts you in a good pocket of ore."

All at once I understood why Nikko's parents had such a nice house. At the same time, I felt bad about the doubts I'd had about Father being a good worker. For no matter how rough things got, I know Father would never pay a bribe to get easy digging.

## July 7

Tonight I asked Father about Mr. Nikkola and the snuff box. He looked surprised and said that he hadn't wanted to speak against Nikko's father, but since I knew about the bribes, he'd be honest. He told me that Mr. Nikkola was "on the other side," meaning he'd do anything to flatter the bosses. Father said that Nikkola even brought the foremen whiskey and cigars at Christmastime.

Father went on to explain that it was hard not giving in to the pressure, because the foremen are always threatening the miners. At the start of a shift the foreman will sometimes stand at the mine entrance with yellow slips in his hand. (Those are the papers that tell a man he's been fired.) As soon as the men see those slips, they bust their backs, hoping that they won't be the ones to lose their jobs.

Father laughed and said that most every time the slips turn out to be blank. According to Father the real firing happens without warning. As a group of fellows are leaving the mine, the foreman will look at his watch and tell the first man in line that if he's in such a hurry to get home, he can stay home permanently. It makes no difference whether it's after quitting time or not.

"The foremen get in trouble if they don't fire a certain number of fellows each month," Father said.

## July 8

Today I found out what real darkness is. It happened when Wally and I were at the end of the Clementine drift. We were heading back to the timber shaft when my candle tipped out of its wire holder and fell into a puddle. Since Wally was saving his own candle — they charge us for each one — everything went black.

I blinked in disbelief at the total darkness. It made no difference if my eyes were closed or open. I felt like a huge door had slammed shut and sucked away every hint of light and shadow. For a moment I felt like shouting. It wasn't until Wally finally scraped a match across the iron wheel of our cart that I realized I'd been holding my breath the whole time.

## July 9

More miners are talking about Socialism and strikes. Father told me to be careful who I talk to, because the company has hired men to spy on their fellow workers. The spies get a dollar a day bonus to report union organizing to the superintendent. The company must really hate the union if they are willing to pay nearly a half a day's wages just to get our names.

I'm not sure what Socialism is, but according to Father it is a way of thinking that says the government should own and operate companies for the good of the people. That way everyone can share in the profits instead of having a handful of rich fellows living at the expense of millions of poor people.

I can't see what's wrong about saying those things out loud, but Father claims any mention of such ideas will get you blacklisted. That means the Oliver not only fires you, but they also send your name to every company in Minnesota and Michigan, so your can't ever work in a mine again.

When I asked Father if he thought Mr. Nikkola might be working as a spy, he said it was "likely."

## July 10

Mother is still worried about my working underground. Though she tries not to show it, her voice quavers every morning when she hands me my lunch pail and tells me to take care.

At quitting time, whether I'm walking home alone or with Father, I can see her standing at the front window, peering toward the mine. But by the time I reach the house, she is busy setting out our supper and pretending that everything is fine.

## July 11

It's usually so noisy underground that you have to yell to talk. There's a constant commotion with the mules jerking along the ore cars, the skip lifting, and the fellows scraping with their shovels and pounding on their drills.

But sometimes it can be eerily quiet. Today we'd just unloaded some timbers in the Jenny Lou, when Wally said, "Listen."

I started to tell him that I couldn't hear a thing, but he hushed me with a wave of his hand.

At first it sounded like a rope being pulled so taut that it was ready to snap. Then I realized it was the timbers creaking under the weight of the earth.

"Do you think . . . ?" Wally stopped.

I told him the engineers must have things figured out, but the truth was that sound chilled me to the marrow. We got out of that drift as fast as we could.

Tonight as I sit beside my oil lamp and write these words, the creaking of those support posts still echoes through my head. All I can do these days is treasure my time above ground.

## July 12

We are finally getting a few fresh vegetables from our garden. Mother made boiled fish and creamed peas and potatoes for supper tonight. I could barely wait for Lisa to finish saying grace before we dug in.

## July 14

In the sauna tonight, Father and his friends started talking about their early days on the Range. Arne Maki said that when he first came to the Mesabi, he worked in a pit where he had to climb down a 175-foot ladder. He said it took forever to get up and down, especially at the end of a shift when he was tired or when the rungs were slippery with ice. "But we was paid portal to portal," he said. (That meant his time on the ladder wasn't counted as time on the job.)

I guess I shouldn't complain about pushing a timber cart.

This evening I started reading a story called "The Hound of the Baskervilles" that Nikko gave me. I was so tired that I fell asleep right in the middle.

## July 15

I am amazed at how smart the mules are at the Helsinki. They can follow orders in Finn, English, Italian, and Slovenian. Father's favorite mule is Sampo (named after a magical mill in a poem called the *Kalevala*). Sampo knows when his ore car is filled, and he starts for the skip before you even tell him.

As clever as the mules are, it riles me to see the foremen treat animals better than us miners. Our only days off are Sundays and Christmas, but the mules get thirty days' vacation in the company pasture every year. If the foremen weren't so worried about the health of the mules, I'd bet they'd have us carting out ore before the blasting dust had even begun to settle.

## July 16

The drought continues. We are hauling water by the bucketful to keep our garden alive. At least the mosquitoes have died.

Every time I see Nikko, I think about his father. Sometimes I feel like asking him if he's heard about the company spying that's going on in the mines, but I never do. Nothing has been proven, so it's only right for me to hold my tongue.

## July 19

The Socialists are getting more outspoken all the time. There is a Finnish boardinghouse in town where they follow the teachings of a man called Antero Tanner. Their goal is to purify their minds and bodies. They drink no coffee. They eat no meat or white bread, and they take cold baths every day. Instead of drinking in the saloons, they go to the Socialist Hall and spend their time discussing political philosophy.

Though it makes sense to eat right and not waste your money on liquor, the cold baths sound crazy. I'd rather take a sauna.

## July 22

Sunday. The whole family went blueberry-picking this afternoon. The dry weather has made for a scarce crop, but I enjoyed getting out into the open air.

Father says the bears will be mean this fall if the hazelnut crop turns out as bad as the berries.

## July 26

It finally happened. We had a cave-in.

Wally and I were bringing a load of timbering to the

raise crew at the far end of the Jenny Lou. One of the fellows had just waved hello, when a rush of air blew out all our candles at once.

Someone shouted, "Run," and as I turned to sprint toward the main shaft, an explosion of dust rolled over me. I ran into the tail end of a mule, who snorted and kicked my legs out from under me. A boot caught me square in the ribs, but I was up and running in a flash.

By the time we stumbled to the main shaft, it was quiet. That meant most of the timbers had held. Wally lit his candle and passed it around. We were all wheezing and coughing.

Just then the cage opened and one of the Cornish foremen, Eli Branscomb, stepped out. A railroad lantern swung from his hand. He had five men with him. They all had shovels and lining bars in their hands, and their pockets were stuffed with extra candles. "Is everyone all right?" Branscomb asked.

One fellow said, "Yes," and then, "No," when he remembered the men at the end of the drift.

Without another word Branscomb tied a handkerchief across his face and headed down the dusty, red tunnel. We trailed right behind, knowing that every minute counted if someone was hurt.

We found three men pinned under a pile of rocks and timbers. We threw the rubble off and helped the fellows brush the dirt out of their faces. Though two of the men were cut up, it didn't look like any bones were broken.

I was studying one of the collapsed posts when I saw the fourth man. It was Reino Lahti, one of our sauna partners, and he was lying curled against the wall like he was asleep.

I called for Branscomb. When the foreman knelt down to check the pulse in Reino's neck, his hand came away bloody. He turned him over, and I couldn't believe my eyes. A splinter from the shattered post had caught him flush in the throat.

Suddenly I was feeling sicker than that night on the ship when the fellow in the hammock above me puked in my face.

By the time we helped the injured fellows to the surface, a crowd had gathered. But before we could talk with anyone, Branscomb said, "You boys better get started with the cleanup."

When Wally and I just stared, he said, "What's the matter? Do I have to say it in Finn, too?"

Climbing into the cage and being lowered back down into that mine was the hardest thing I've ever done.

All afternoon I kept thinking about the times that Wally and I had passed by the very place where those timbers had exploded. The question is, where and when will it happen next?

"You're quitting," was the first thing that Mother said when I got home.

I was ready to agree until I thought it over. It was easy to quit, but what would come next? Would Father quit, too? We couldn't move back to Finland. We couldn't afford a farm yet.

No matter which way I looked at things, the answer was always the same — for now the Oliver Iron Mining Company owned me lock, stock, and barrel.

## August 1

Some leaders from the American Socialist Party led a big rally today. Father is excited about a new group they are organizing called the Finnish Socialist Federation. After parading down Pine Street, they set up a barrel and took turns giving speeches. Comrade Halonen spoke on the themes of Socialism. Then a representative of the Western Federation of Miners, Teofilo Petriella, gave a loud talk in Italian that got everybody clapping and cheering.

A picnic is set for Penobscot Grove on Sunday. Father doesn't like to go around calling people "comrade" like these fellows do — he says "mister is more rank than a regular fellow needs" — but he knows that the Socialists back labor one hundred percent. Though Mother calls it blasphemy, Father jokes that he'd join up with the devil himself if it would help him start a union.

## August 2

I cashed my paycheck and gave every cent to Mother for her money jar. After the cave-in, I want to get clear of this town as fast as I can.

These days, every time a timber creaks I think back to Reino Lahti lying with that splinter through his neck.

## August 7

Still no rain.

## August 8

The Socialist Party met all week at Tapio Hall, the headquarters of the local Temperance Society. People came from all over the United States, and there were huge crowds every day. The party signed up over 2,000 people.

Though Father is generally not a joiner, he enrolled with the Socialists because he believes they are the only group that has a chance of organizing a union on the Range. Mr. Halonen — or should I say Comrade? — told him that Hibbing will soon be the largest foreign-language

Socialist group in America. There are rumors that the Russian Czar has sent members of his secret police to Hibbing to spy on the meeting, but Father says that is nonsense.

## August 9

Today I took Lisa to the Greater Norris and Rowe Tented Circus. (Helena went with Helmi Nikkola and paid for her own admission with money she earned at Lamppa's boardinghouse.) I was tired from the night shift, but when I leaned back to take a nap, Lisa poked my shoulder and said, "You don't want to miss this." She pointed to a bareback rider named Edna Maretta, who is the only person in the world who can do a backward somersault on a galloping horse. I thanked her for pointing out the trick, but I dozed off again during the elephant act.

## August 10

Since I've been working at the Helsinki, I notice things about nature that I took for granted before. And it's not just sunshine. It's little things like the song of a meadowlark ringing out pure and clear, the scent of fresh-cut hay in the field by Penobscot Grove, and the maple leaves, flickering with a hundred shades of green all at once.

It's a lot like the myth about Persephone being freed from the kingdom of Hades each spring. Only my spring comes after each and every shift in the mine.

## August 12

Nikko and I went fishing in a creek north of the Pool Location this afternoon. We didn't catch a thing because even the deepest holes had dried up to puddles.

I keep telling myself that it's not Nikko's fault his father is a snitch.

## August 23

The drought has finally ended. It started raining on Monday about 9:00 in the evening, and it never stopped until Wednesday. For once I will not complain about mud or bugs.

## September 4

This afternoon a charge went off in the Clementine drift just as four men were returning to their work site. Arvo Nurmi got a rock chip in his eye, but no one else was hurt.

Just when I think Helena is growing up, she goes and

acts spoiled again. Ever since she saw an ad for a "clothing carnival" at Kero's store, she's been begging Mother for a store-bought dress.

All Lisa gets are Helena's hand-me-downs, which were only made out of flour sacks in the first place, but she never complains.

## September 21

According to the *Mesaba Ore,* a big typhoon has hit Hong Kong, killing 50,000 people. Mother wanted to send some money over there, but we just don't have any to spare. Instead, she and her suffragette friends collected four boxes of clothing and blankets.

## September 25

Miss Wilders surprised me with a nice letter saying how sorry she was that I hadn't been able to attend classes this year. She invited me to return if "my circumstances changed."

I wrote a note back (using my pencil so I didn't have to worry about blots and smudges). I told her about my journal and the books I've read, and I promised to keep practicing my English.

## October 7

Today Nikko and I went to the St. Louis County Fair that had traveled to Hibbing. We saw every kind of vegetable, animal, preserve, and pie that you could imagine. Father met a homesteader named Andrew Mattson from a place up north called Bear River, and he asked him a million questions about the farms.

My favorite event was the horse race. The day reminded me of the winter races we had on Lake Ähtärinjärvi back in Lehtimäki. Father and I both miss those Sunday afternoons. Father is certain that cars will never replace horses, because, in his words, cars are nothing but "noise and confusion."

## October 20

James J. Hill, the railroad millionaire from St. Paul, has agreed to lease his ore properties to United States Steel. According to the paper, the ore is valued at 400 million dollars, making it the largest business deal in the history of America.

Father wonders if all that money will allow the company to take better care of the widows and orphans of the miners who've been killed. Right now the death and disability payments are so low that many of the widows are forced to work as saloon gals to support their kids.

## November 1

Though our wages are not improving at the mine, Father has found a new way to make extra money. It all started when Mrs. Nikkola noticed the toy train that Father had carved for Lisa. She hired him to make one for her nephew, and it turned out so nice that she bragged it up to her neighbor Mrs. Jarvela, who told a friend of hers. Before he knew it, Father had a dozen orders to make trains for Christmas presents. He's not charging much, but he says that every nickel will count toward the purchase of our farm.

## November 2

Nikko has been reading a book called *The Jungle.* It sounded like an exciting story about Africa, but when he told me that it described a meat-packing plant I was disappointed. Still he insisted on reading it out loud. He said his mother's cousin works for a newspaper called *The Appeal to Reason,* which paid the author, Mr. Upton Sinclair, $500 so he could write the book.

When Nikko started reading, I couldn't believe my ears. According to Mr. Sinclair, the meat packers in Chicago don't give a lick about cleanliness. The meat is old and covered with flies, they sell goat as lamb chops, and what's worse, the stuff they call deviled ham is actually a mixture of tripe (that's the stomach of an animal) stirred up with sausage and lard. That same recipe has been known to contain the remains of workers who have fallen into the boiling vat! When I told Nikko it sounded like a big lie, he said Mr. Sinclair spent two months at the stockyards to make sure that he found out the truth.

I asked him to quit right there, because it was time for me to go home and eat lunch. Nikko says he hasn't eaten a speck of meat since he got to the description of hog butchering in chapter three. I can't blame him.

## November 4

I told Mother and Father to not waste money buying me birthday presents, but they gave me a box of 30:30 shells and a freshly minted silver dollar anyway. Despite Mother's protests, I dropped the dollar into her homestead jar.

## November 10

Though some of the mines are staying in production all winter, the owners of the Helsinki have decided to shut down next week. Father says the layoff will give us a chance to put our toy-making shop into full production, but I know he's worried that this could be a rough winter without our wages from the mine.

Just when we were beginning to set a few pennies aside, the layoffs come. It sure puts a damper on Christmas.

## November 24

Only a few more days of deer season are left. Hunting has been rough because of all the snow and cold weather. The Sturgeon Lake country already has a foot of snow on the ground. Father and I are lucky we got our deer on opening weekend.

## November 28

A banker in town has hired Father to build a wooden model of a "laker," one of the big boats that haul ore from Duluth to the steel plants out east. This fellow was a seaman when he was young, and he gets lonesome for the

Great Lakes. He told Father to take his time and not worry about how much it will cost!

Another rich fellow has asked him to carve a duck decoy out of cedar to set on his fireplace mantel.

The Power-Simpson people want Father to work at the mill, too. He sure is going to be busy with all the projects he has to finish. As a joke, Father said that if he's not careful his Socialist friends will be calling him a capitalist.

## November 29

We had our second Thanksgiving dinner in America. Like last year we had baked venison, partridge (compliments of me), and wild rice (thanks to Mother's Ojibwa friend). Though the year was poor for blueberries, Mother canned enough so we could have our pie.

I like the American idea of setting aside a day for thanks. When I think of all the men on the Mesabi who've been killed or crippled in accidents, I know I'm lucky to still be in one piece.

## December 7

It was twenty below zero this morning. Father has just heard about a new college in Duluth that is dedicated to the principles of Socialism. It's called the Work People's College. He wishes that he could afford to send me there.

But even if he had the money, I'd have to finish high school first, and that doesn't seem possible anymore.

## December 13

Another bad snowstorm. The trains are running late. Even though winter doesn't officially start for another week, I'm already sick of shoveling snow. The folks who print calendars should make separate ones for Minnesota.

Father and I have been building toys like crazy. I do the rough shaping and Father does the detailed carving. Helena and Lisa help with the painting. Though Lisa is a bit messy at times, Helena touches things up for her. Father teases Helena and asks if she is just being nice so she can get a good Christmas present.

It is too bad that I am working above ground now that the weather has turned cold. The mine with its constant fifty-degree temperature feels good when it's twenty and thirty below.

Father has put a barrel stove in his workshop, but even when it's stoked up with wood scraps, the corners stay cold. We bring the paint cans into the house at night to keep them from freezing.

## December 17

Father got a letter from Andrew Mattson, the Bear River farmer who he met at the county fair last fall. Mattson told Father that a good piece of land will be coming up for sale in the spring. According to his letter, the farm is run-down but cheap — only $350 — and he is sure that the widow lady who owns it would hold a contract for deed if Father can come up with a down payment.

We are all excited. If Father had his way, he would hike up to Bear River tomorrow and look the place over, but he is writing a letter instead.

I know Mother was thinking about dipping into her money jar to buy Christmas presents, but I told her that we'd be better off having a lean Christmas and leaving our homestead fund alone. The girls both agreed and told her that some hand-knitted mittens and caps would suit them just fine.

## December 18

Nikko lent me a new Christmas story by a writer named O. Henry. It is called "The Gift of the Magi," and it tells about a poor young couple who use their last pennies to buy each other Christmas presents. The ending is a real surprise. Nikko says that all O. Henry's stories have little twists like that.

## December 25

We did our best to act pleased when we opened our handmade presents. Helena surprised me the most. Not only did she give Mother a big hug and kiss for the sweater, but she also washed all the dishes after dinner.

But the whole time we were doing without, I kept thinking about the big pile of presents under Mr. Nikkola's tree. I hope Mr. Nikkola chokes on the fat goose that he's roasting.

## December 29

Though Christmas has come and gone, Mrs. Nikkola is still bragging up Father's woodcarving talents. She calls Father a genius, but he says he's just happy that he doesn't cut himself very often.

Her talking must be doing some good, because he's got orders from as far away as Eveleth and Gilbert. Not too long ago he was worried about us going hungry during his layoff, but now he has more projects than there are hours in the day.

## January 1, 1907

I can't believe that it's already 1907. I always used to be in a rush for everything to happen, but now I'd be happier if time would slow down a notch. If only I was in school like Nikko. Then I could read and study while I waited for that one special thing to catch my fancy. But I know it's just not possible.

## January 18

Mrs. Seppala, the lady with the homestead in Bear River, wrote back to Father and said that she would be happy to show him her farm. We are going to look at it next month after the cold weather has broken.

## January 27

The wife of the superintendent of the Susquehanna mine has hired Father to build a wooden replica of a Model 60 Marion steam shovel. She wants to give it to her son as a birthday present.

Father says it feels like robbery to take money for building play toys, but he smiles whenever he drops a coin in Mother's jar.

## February 20

Father borrowed a sleigh from his friend, Riika Koskela, and we took the Green-Rock road up to Mrs. Seppala's farm. Since the road only opened up two years ago, it is still rough in places. The hard-packed snow makes traveling easy, but I wouldn't want to try it once the mud holes and the corduroy sections (where logs are laid side by side) thaw out.

Bear River isn't much more than a wide spot in the trail with a tiny log post office, a schoolhouse, and a store called Waechter and Amundson's. As small as the town is, Father was excited to hear that a fellow named John Hayden has already started a newspaper called the *Bear River Journal.*

Though Mrs. Seppala's place is set on a pretty piece of ground, it needs lots of work. The rail fences have fallen down, the fields are overgrown with alder brush, and the barn needs major repair. But the log house and sauna look plumb and solid.

While Father and I walked the property lines, Mother and the girls had coffee with Mrs. Seppala. She wants to stay on the farm for the summer but said we were welcome to take over in the fall. She agreed to $100 down as soon as Father could get the money together and said she'd hold the $250 balance on a contract for deed.

Father offered to pay interest, but she said that she'd rather see a nice family move into her place than "quibble over a few pennies."

## March 1

Father and I have been called back to work at the mine, but we are still continuing our toy making after work and on Sundays. Mother's money jar is finally filling up again.

Like so many of the small mines in the area, the Helsinki has been bought by the Oliver Iron Mining Company. That makes us employees of United States Steel, which Father does not like at all.

## March 3

Father has invited me to partner with him as a contract miner. He says if I'm going to work underground, I might as well be making the extra wages of a miner. He said we'll both be "short timers" anyway, meaning that if everything goes well, we'll be on our farm in the fall.

## March 5

Mining is a lot tougher than timber tramming. In some places Father and I just knock the ore loose with a pick-axe or a lining bar and shovel it in the tram car, but in other places the rock is so hard that it takes half a shift to make one dynamite hole. I'm getting so tall that I have to work hunched over, and swinging a sledgehammer to drive the drill rods just about breaks my back.

By lunchtime my ears are ringing from hitting steel. Father's attitude gets us stuck working the hardest rock, but there is no changing him. I can understand him not paying bribes — I won't do that either — but he could at least say good morning to the foreman. Whenever I suggest that he be more polite to the bosses, he says, "Keep your sermons to yourself."

## March 8

Nikko stopped by to visit this evening, and as usual, he brought the girls a treat. We have less in common these days, but we always have our books to chat about. Right now we are both reading short stories by Jack London.

## March 10

When Carlson is on duty at the mine, I can understand Father's negative attitude toward the foremen. This morning as Father and I were approaching the main entrance, he jeered and called us a "pair of darkies." Then after we walked past his snuff box without putting a coin in, he spoke to the fellows behind us, saying, "Too bad those Mongols won't go back where they came from and leave us white folks alone."

When I think of all the abuse Father has taken from that man just to keep food on our table, I have to admire his self-control. I would have smacked the fool long ago.

## March 23

Today's *Mesaba Ore* spoke out against the Western Federation of Miners. The editors called Petriella "a black-hearted rascal."

Now I know what happens when a man has the courage to speak out against the local politicians and mine officials. As much as Father loves his paper, he is ready to cancel his subscription.

## April 1

There is more talk among the miners about joining the union. Though it is strictly done in whispers to avoid getting fired, the men know that the peak of the ore shipping season is their only chance to put pressure on the company. At the last Socialist Hall meeting Father got up and said, "The only way to get the attention of Mr. Rockefeller and Mr. Carnegie is by calling an all-out strike."

Even though Father is doing all he can to help the union, he is placing his real faith in our homestead. He still knows that the land is our only hope. *Oma tupa, oma lupa*.

## April 11

Father just wrote a letter to Mrs. Seppala and told her we would have the down payment by early summer. I was proud when Mother said my wages are really helping fill the money jar.

## April 13

I think the bosses at the Helsinki have heard that Father is attending meetings in the Socialist Hall, because we have been assigned to the worst place ever in the mine. Not only is the drilling tough, but there are live springs everywhere. Even with the pumps running steady, we are standing in puddles of water.

✣ ✣ ✣

## April 27

Andrew Carnegie has given Hibbing a $25,000 grant to build a public library. As much as I love books, I can not figure out why Carnegie would spend his whole life robbing money from poor people and then give it back. Mother says he probably has a guilty conscience. Wouldn't it have been a whole lot simpler to pay his workers a fair wage so they could build their own libraries?

## April 28

It's supposed to be spring, but we just got a foot of snow! The wind blew so hard that the drifts are three and four feet deep. Several ships were lost on the Great Lakes.

## May 20

Nikko and I have been going fishing nearly every evening for the last two weeks. Even when I'm dead tired from my shift, the spring air livens me up. And after a long winter of canned venison and jerky, the fresh fish is a welcome change. Mother's been cooking walleye every way you can imagine: fried, boiled, baked, smoked, and pickled. Lisa has come to Mahoning Pond with us a few times, and she always catches her share.

## June 8

The Miles Vaudeville Theater opened up this week, and it is the fanciest building I have ever seen. Though I can't afford to go to a show, Nikko and I looked inside. The whole front is polished brass, marble, and French plate glass. The trim is oak and mahogany (what Father could do with fine wood like that!) and the seats are plush velvet. The arch above the stage is decorated with fancy plaster work and framed by gold-roped curtains that would make even a second-rate performer look first class.

## June 9

Father and I are now working in the Agnes drift, the newest and wettest level in the mine. Father jokes about us turning into fish, but I have reached the end of my patience. I'm tired of mining more mud than iron ore.

Now that the weather has warmed up, it's harder than ever to step into that damp, rusty cage. Every morning I try to hang on to the sound of the bird calls and the scent of the grass, but it all flashes away in the instant that I'm lowered into the mine.

Today I split my thumb open with the sledgehammer. My hands were so cold that the hammer slipped out of my hand. When I reached down to catch it, my thumb got crushed against the rail. Thick drops of black blood splashed onto my boot, but all I could do was wrap the cut with my handkerchief and keep pounding on the drill rod. When will I escape this mine where it is forever night and forever winter?

I feel like I don't belong in this town. I keep thinking back to the green summers that I spent on Grandpa's farm. Things were so clean and simple and calm. Now it seems like the Old Country has forgotten me, and the new one doesn't care.

## June 15

According to the paper, the stock of United States Steel is now valued at over one billion dollars, making it the first billion-dollar corporation in U.S. history.

How can a company worth a billion dollars pay us only $2.50 per day, less supplies?

✣ ✣ ✣

## June 20

Norway and Austria have added their names to the list of countries who have given women the right to vote. Mother can't believe that America is lagging so far behind. She says we shouldn't pretend to be a democracy if half the people aren't allowed to have a say.

Mother still says she will take citizenship classes as soon as women get the right to vote.

## June 24

Our whole family went to a midsummer picnic sponsored by the Finnish Temperance Society. It was meant to be a quiet sort of American Juhannus Day, but some radical Socialists got up and started complaining about the steel companies. They told us that we were "slaves of the steel trust" and that all the politicians were owned by the mining companies.

Though the Socialists were shouted down by more moderate Temperance people, I could see lots of miners in the crowd nodding their heads. For there is no way you can work in the heart of a cold black mine ten hours at a stretch, six days a week, and not feel like a slave.

## June 29

The high school graduating class was up to twelve this year, the largest in the history of Hibbing. I promised Nikko I would watch him when he marches across the stage next year. His grades rank him at the top of his class.

Sometimes I wonder how well I could have done if I'd stayed in school, but would I want to trade away an honest father to get what Nikko has?

## July 2

Father signed the papers to buy the Seppala farm today. Before he left for the bank this morning, Lisa reminded him to tell Mrs. Seppala that she could come and visit us anytime. Ever since we agreed to buy the farm, Lisa has been worried that Mrs. Seppala will get lonesome for her old house.

## July 4

Today Hibbing sponsored their biggest Fourth of July celebration ever.

Though it was too wet to have the horse races, the baseball game went on as scheduled. Hibbing lost to a Minneapolis team. Nikko says that if Hibbing had a few

Finns on their team they would be twice as good. (He still insists I'm good enough to play.) Later we watched some Cornish wrestling matches. Branscomb, the brawny foreman from our mine, took his man without even getting up a sweat.

For the grand finale they lit up the sky over the Rust pit with fireworks.

## July 10

Father has been meeting with the other fellows who joined the Western Federation union. They are getting ready to organize a strike, but he says it needs to be a surprise.

## July 16

Tonight when Father and I were working in the garden, tying up the tomato vines, Ed Finnila pulled up in a wagon and jumped down all out of breath. He told Father that the workers at the loading docks in Duluth had started a wildcat strike.

"Dammit," Father shouted, kicking the ground with his boot heel and breaking a tomato stake in half. Father never swears within earshot of Mother or the girls, who were darning socks on the front porch, but this time he yelled loud enough for the neighbors to hear. Father said that if the Oliver can't ship any ore, they won't care if we strike till Christmas.

I wanted to tell him to keep his hopes up, but when I looked down and saw how deep his boot had buried that stake in the ground, I knew we were stuck in a very bad place.

## July 17

Father has been to three union meetings in the last two days. Rather than waiting for wildcat strikes to start all over the Range, the union has decided to offer the company fair terms.

## July 18

The Oliver has refused to meet with the union.

## July 19

The Western Federation of Miners sent a list of demands to the Oliver Iron Mining Company today. After talking late into the night, the union voted to keep their list short but to stick with it no matter what.

The miners are asking for three things:

1. An eight-hour day.
2. Wages of $2.50 per day in the pits and $3.00 underground.
3. Elimination of bribes to foremen.

Since only a fourth of the 10,000 miners on the Range belong to the union (and Father says that less than 700 of those fellows are active), Petriella is hoping to organize every worker in the Mesabi district by passing out bylaws of the "Constitution of the Minnesota District Union Number 11 of the Western Federation of Miners."

Pickets are set to take their places at every mine if the Oliver superintendent doesn't respond by midnight.

Father gave Carlson the shock of his life today. Our shift started with Carlson spouting the same ugly talk he always does. He asked Father if it was sauna smoke that made him so black, but Father acted totally deaf.

After our shift was done, Carlson was sitting on a stool near the entrance to the cage. As the miners pushed past him, Carlson singled out Father and said that it was too bad that the spring water hadn't washed all his dirt off.

Without saying a word, Father walked over to Carlson

and stopped. The other miners turned as Father put his big fist in front of Carlson's nose. Hanging on to his stool with a white-knuckled grip, the foreman leaned back, wide-eyed.

Father opened his hand and showed a shiny half dollar. "Get out your snuffbox, Mr. Samuel Everett Carlson," Father said. Carlson was stunned that Father was speaking English. "Because once this strike starts you're gonna need this a hell of a lot more than me."

Then Father flipped the heavy coin with his thumb. It hit Carlson in the bridge of his nose and clanged to the ground. When Carlson bent over to pick up the coin, Father kicked him square in the rear. The miners roared as Carlson pitched face forward onto the ground and his snuffbox spilled open.

Carlson was still on his knees, scrambling to catch his coins, as Father and I turned to walk through the gate of the Helsinki for the last time.

## July 20

The Oliver fired 300 miners today. It was no surprise when Father's name was on the list. Father claims that being fired is good because it will hurry along our farming plans.

What upsets me most is that the company is ignoring the union demands altogether. Father said the Oliver superintendent laughed at our list. Pointing to the request for cutting out bribes, he said, "Our foremen need the extra money. They have lots of children to feed."

Father had hoped that if the miners were reasonable, they could reach a quick settlement. But the Oliver has chosen to pretend that the union doesn't exist.

After all the tons of ore we've drilled and blasted, the company is now saying that we aren't even worth talking to. What about all the accidents that made women into widows? What about the babies who will grow up without ever knowing their fathers?

I get so mad when I think about it that I'd like to give that Oliver superintendent a good crack with a lining bar.

## July 21

Even as we are standing at the locked gates of the mine with our picket signs, Father is keeping his eye on the dock strike in Duluth. There's no sign of a settlement down there, and I suspect the mining companies want to keep it that way.

The Socialist Hall is being used as a strike office. Mother and the other ladies have stocked the tables with fresh baked goods and hot coffee. The women and children organized a march all on their own. Lisa and Helena printed up a sign that read GIVE OUR FATHERS A FAIR DEAL.

## July 22

Father heard from Louis Jenkins, a friend who works in the Oliver accounting department, that the company is bringing in special deputies to intimidate the strikers. What scares me most is that Jenkins says the company has also placed orders for German Lugers and ammunition.

I sure hope things don't turn crazy like they did out in Cripple Creek, Colorado, where all those miners were killed.

## July 23

This morning Petriella led 600 or 700 of us on a march to a vacant lot on the corner of Penobscot Road and First Avenue. He climbed on a stump and told us that we were fighting for the rights of working men everywhere, and that if we stuck together we could teach the steel trust a lesson.

When we got back to the Hall, a photographer had set

up a camera to take a picture of Petriella. After the fellow was done, he surprised me by asking if he could photograph a "regular" miner like me. Though I was nervous, I did my best to smile.

## July 24

Things are looking worse every day.

The Oliver has decided to bring in replacement workers from out East. Father heard that they are mainly Montenegrins and Croats who have just arrived in America. Not only are they hungry for jobs, but since they don't know English, they will have no idea that they are being hired to break a strike.

## July 27

There was an open meeting at the Power Theater for citizens who are concerned about the strike. The town invited five representatives of the WFM — Father was one of them — to appear.

I figured most people would support the miners, but I have never been more wrong. Two village councilors started things off by calling the WFM a bloodthirsty and murderous organization. Then Herman Antonelli, speaking in both English and Italian, condemned the WFM some more. Next a man, alternating between English and Slovenian, did the same thing.

The worst speech of all was delivered by H. R. Weirick, Hibbing's village president. He issued a proclamation forbidding marches and demonstrations of any kind, and he even authorized the citizens to act as deputies in breaking up public disturbances. That made everyone a self-appointed vigilante.

I was dumbfounded when I saw the anger in that crowd. How could businessmen condemn the very people who had been supporting their stores since the town was founded? Without the trade of the miners, not a single one of them could survive, yet they refused to even consider that we might deserve a fifty-cent-a-day raise.

When the WFM spokesman finally had his chance to talk, the crowd ignored his every word. Without any further discussion, they voted a resolution refusing to recognize the WFM. Father's shoulders slumped as the union fellows got up to leave the hall. The crowd hooted and jeered like they were at a prizefight. I felt my temper flare. By denying our very existence, the village had delivered the same insult as the Oliver.

When the door swung shut behind Father, I stood up. Half the audience turned in my direction. I heard one pasty-faced storekeeper whisper, "There's one of 'em."

I drew in a deep breath and stared right at him. Though I felt like shouting, I talked just loud enough for everyone in the auditorium to hear. "Who's gonna buy your flour and beans now?" I said. "Who's gonna go to your fancy vaudeville shows?" Then I stepped into the aisle and walked straight out the same door as Father without ever turning my head.

How I would like to take every one of those fat businessmen down into the deepest hellhole in the Helsinki and have them hammer on a steel drill for ten hours straight.

## July 28

Yesterday the *Mesaba Ore* printed its worst attack yet on our union. They said that the WFM is ninety percent Finlanders who are followers of the red flag. They went on to call Petriella a "festering putrid ulcer," an "alien Dago anarchist," and an "unmitigated, vicious, venomous liar."

Father has written a letter canceling his subscription.

## July 30

The replacement workers are arriving. Though Father won't admit it in public, he knows there isn't much chance for the strike to succeed without the town's support. But he is already looking forward to living in the country where the steel trust won't be owning him any more.

## August 1

As if things haven't been going bad enough, the police arrested Petriella today. The charge was carrying a concealed weapon, but everyone knows the real reason — the mining companies control the police, and they hope to break the strike by putting our leader in jail.

## August 2

Businessmen across the Iron Range are refusing to extend credit to the miners. Finns are being turned down more than any other group, because we have been branded as radicals.

So Mother and Father and a bunch of other Finnish families have decided to start a cooperative store. The plan is to pool all our grocery money and order food from the wholesalers in Duluth. Then we can sell it at cost to our members.

## August 8

Father bought a Kentucky-style farm wagon and a horse from a man in Penobscot who is moving to St. Paul. He and I hauled a wagonload of things to Bear River this morning, while Mother and the girls stayed in Hibbing to help out at strike headquarters. Father figures it will take two or three more trips for us to get everything moved. We left town before dawn and got to the farm by late morning. After storing our things in the sauna, we spent the whole day working on the barn. Father says that he plans on using this barn for our horses. One day he hopes to build a bigger one for dairy cattle.

Mrs. Seppala made us a fine lunch. She says she loves to hear the sound of our saw and hammers. Father invited her to come and visit after she moves to Cook next month, and she said, "I just may do that, boys."

Her calling Father a boy made me grin, but I guess she is old enough to be his mother.

## August 10

Nineteen Finns were arrested for picketing outside Rukavina's boardinghouse near the Burt mine. They tried to block the boarders, who are mainly Austrian, from going to work.

## August 15

In their latest effort to break the strike, the Oliver is pressuring the grocery wholesalers to refuse delivery to our new Co-op Store. The same thing is happening all across the Range. Mother and her friends have raised enough money to set up an account, yet no one will take their order.

Three hundred Montenegrin strikebreakers arrived by train today.

## August 17

It was only a matter of time before it happened. Company "detectives" fired into a group of strikers at the Rust mine shaft and wounded a man. We don't know if he's going to live or not.

Even as things are getting more violent, the local baseball team keeps playing. In their latest four-game series Hibbing split with the St. Paul Colored Gophers.

## August 24

Mother Jones, the famous labor leader, has come to Hibbing in support of our strike. She gave a rousing speech about how the miners on the Mesabi are treated like slaves, but I fear it's too late to help. A good crowd showed up to hear Miss Jones, which is surprising since there are spies watching us all of the time.

According to Father, the Oliver pays the spies, who are our neighbors and co-workers, to turn in the names of miners who are going to strike meetings. The company then prints up a "blacklist," which labels them as trouble-makers and warns other superintendents not to hire them.

The Western Federation president has returned to Denver.

## August 30

The Oliver has brought in more than a thousand strike-breakers this month. Whenever I start to feel hatred toward those men, I have to remind myself that it isn't their fault. They are being used by the company and have no idea that they are putting honest men out of work.

Father heard that the Oliver is placing ads in the papers out East, asking for more workers. They want men right off the boats who don't know about the strike. They lock the fellows up in a train and haul them straight to Minnesota under armed guard. One of our Montenegrin union men spoke through the fence to a fellow, who said he was afraid that he was being hauled off to fight as a soldier in some war.

The Oliver keeps the Montenegrins in camps away from town, so no one can tell them the truth. The company has built big bunk shacks on the mine property, and they keep the work sites under guard. When our men try to shout over the fences and explain about the strike, the Oliver thugs beat up our guys with clubs and haul them off to jail. Since the village president Weirick has proclaimed that anyone can declare himself a deputy, we have no way to fight these illegal arrests.

## September 1

More people are leaving town every day. Mother talked to a storekeeper in Hibbing who said that every suitcase, trunk, and pack sack has been sold out for weeks.

## September 10

The mines are nearly back to full production. Most everyone has given up and gone back to work. The only holdouts are us Finns and a few Italian Socialists.

Hundreds of Finns have been blacklisted. Not only has word spread across the Mesabi Range, but mines on the Vermilion and Cuyuana Ranges have been told as well. Father heard that some of our names have been sent to mines as far away as Montana and West Virginia. Since Father was never shy about speaking his mind, I suspect his name is at the head of every list.

The big surprise was Mr. Nikkola. Nikko said that when his father reported back to the mine, the foreman said there was no work available. He tried another mine, and they told him the same thing. The third place said straight out that they weren't hiring any Finns because they were all agitators and reds.

Since Mr. Nikkola never supported the union, I thought Father might enjoy hearing that he'd been blacklisted, but it made him sad. Father said that though he'd never respected Nikkola, no man deserved to be labeled. "Companies and governments should stand clear of a man's private beliefs," he said.

## September 11

More household goods are going up for sale every day as families leave town. Folks like us who are heading to the country have it easy compared to the people who are moving to cities. They can't take half of their things with them. With so many people leaving, everything is selling cheap. Over the last week we've used Father's toy money to buy a dairy cow, a plow, and lots of hand tools.

Though most of the folks are moving to other cities in the Midwest, some are traveling as far as Oregon. A few like the Nikkolas are moving back to Finland.

## September 17

School reopened yesterday. Though it's hard for me to walk by the high school knowing that I will never have a chance to finish my education, it's even harder for Nikko. Now that his father is laid off, he has to work full-time to help out. Nikko won't even go near the south side of town, because seeing the new high school tears him up inside.

These days Nikko is working as a butcher's helper at Cash's Meat Market and doing his best to help his family save up money to pay for their passage back to Vaasa. I couldn't understand why the Nikkolas are moving all the way back to Finland, but Father says they have no choice. According to Father, lots of the miners found out Nikkola was a spy and several have threatened to kill him.

## September 19

The servant girls across the Mesabi are trying to start a union. Their wages, which average $25 per month, are so low that many young girls are turning away from honest work to find jobs in the bars and bawdy houses.

I hope they have better luck than we miners did.

## September 20

Now that Petriella has been released from jail and left town, our last hope is gone. Petriella said he's got important union organizing to do out East, but I suspect he's given up like the rest of us.

## September 21

We are moving to Bear River tomorrow morning. Helmi and Nikko had supper at our house tonight so we could say good-bye. The girls were doing fine at first, but once Helmi started crying, Helena joined in with twice the volume. I told Nikko I hadn't heard wailing that loud since the morning we were leaving Lehtimäki and I had to pry Helena loose from my grandma's waist.

## September 22

We arrived at our homestead just before lunchtime. Mrs. Seppala had left a note that said, "Welcome to your new home," along with the old saying, "*Oma lupa, oma tupa,*" which brought a big smile to Father's face. Mrs. Seppala had left the key on the kitchen table along with some freshly baked *pulla,* my favorite sweet rolls.

## September 23

I can't believe how quiet it is on our farm. With no dynamite blasts popping off and no train whistles screeching last night, I had trouble getting to sleep.

It was only after an owl hooted down by the barn that I realized I was being bothered by the quiet. Then I had to grin at my own foolishness. As I eased back and breathed in the scent of meadow grass and wildflowers rising from beneath my window, I realized all those fretful months back in Finn Town had been worth it. For though we may be an ocean away from Lehtimäki, I feel like we have finally come home to Grandpa Rantala's farm. And with all of the open land in this country, Grandma and Grandpa may be able to join us someday.

## September 26

A fellow at the post office told Father and me that the folks out East are getting ready to test a wireless telegraph. They plan to send a message through the air all the way from America to Ireland. It took us better than a week to travel that far by steamship, yet the words will flash across the ocean in a fraction of a second.

## September 30

This morning Father and I took the wagon to Hibbing to buy some twine and chicken wire. The town is dead compared to last summer when we were marching in the streets. The shopkeepers are wearing their same smug I'm-better-than-you-are smiles, and the mines are trying to make up for the strike by putting out as much ore as they can before the shipping season closes for the winter.

While Father was at the store, I stopped by and visited Nikko. He's got his ticket for Finland now, and he promised to say hello to my grandma and grandpa the first time he gets near Lehtimäki.

Since Nikko can only bring one trunk on the steamship, he offered to give me his books. I refused until he said that he would only get a few pennies for them at the secondhand store.

Then I told him that I would keep his books with the understanding that he could come and get them after he finished engineering school.

As soon as I saw the look on his face, I was sorry I'd mentioned school. I could tell that he hadn't thought about his education for a long time. But it's my hope that he's only temporarily discouraged, and once he gets back to Finland his old fire for learning will return.

When Father came back, we loaded four peach crates full of books into the wagon. Nikko tried to give me his Mark Twain novels, but since there is no writer better than Twain at cheering a fellow up, I made him keep those.

As we rode down Third Avenue on our way out of town, I could see that Hibbing was the same flat, treeless place it had been on the day we'd first arrived. Despite the paved streets and new brick buildings, red dust still sifts out of the sky, and the open pit mines grow wider and deeper. If the Oliver has its way, they'll probably mine the ore right out from under the town one day.

A clerk waved from the doorway of the Itasca Bazaar, but I didn't feel like waving back. I agree with Father, who says the shopkeepers in Hibbing should all stop their pretending and put up the same sign on every store: PROPERTY OF UNITED STATES STEEL. For in my mind, the strike of 1907 proved that all the businessmen and politicians and policemen in this town are nothing but puppets, dancing to the tune of the Oliver Iron Mining Company.

## October 1

Today Father picked up a copy of the Chisholm paper — he swears that he will never buy a *Mesaba Ore* again. The big news is that a million immigrants have come to America since the first of the year. The experts are predicting that an all-time immigration record will be set by year's end.

It amazes me to think about all those folks steaming toward these shores. Each and every one of them is wondering what shape their new lives will take. I only hope for their sake that they don't have to battle too hard before they find a good, solid home like we have.

# Epilogue

✣ ✣ ✣

In 1917, Otto married a girl from Cook named Millie Sippola. When America entered World War I, Otto enlisted in the army and served under General Pershing in Europe. Otto distinguished himself in battle during the summer of 1918, and in September he was wounded in the leg by machine-gun fire during the Battle of the Argonne in France. Though he recovered quickly and returned home two days before Christmas, he walked with a limp for the rest of his life.

When Congress passed the nineteenth Amendment in 1920, granting women's suffrage, Otto's mother followed through on her promise to become an American citizen. However, Otto's father never applied for citizenship, and he insisted on speaking Finnish at home and with his neighbors until the end of his life.

To supplement his farm income after the war, Otto worked part-time at a cooperative store in Sturgeon, Minnesota. The member-owned store sold groceries, hardware, and clothing, and Otto was eventually elected to serve on the board of directors.

Otto also started a small logging operation in Bear River, and with his father's help, built a combination saw mill/lumberyard that supplied building materials for the rapidly growing community. The business also provided jobs for Otto's three sons and offered his father an ideal selection for his wood-carving stock.

Andrew Mattson, the farmer who encouraged Otto's father to buy land in Bear River, continued to promote the community, and he remained a model citizen for the rest of his life. However, one day at the lumber mill he admitted to Otto that he'd murdered a man in Texas and had moved to northern Minnesota to escape the law. Otto kept Mattson's secret, but the authorities finally tracked Mattson down, when he was on his deathbed. After seeing how completely Mattson had reformed his life, they decided to allow him to die in peace.

Otto's parents lived out their lives in Bear River. His father worked the farm until he was seventy-two years old. In his "retirement" Mr. Peltonen enjoyed carving wooden toys for his grandchildren and for the children in the neighborhood, while Mrs. Peltonen continued to keep a big garden. The two of them stayed on the homestead, while Otto, who bought the adjoining farm, worked their land for them. His father died in the spring of 1939, and his mother lived only three months longer.

Otto's sister Helena became one of the first barnstorming female pilots in America. Traveling with her husband, an airplane mechanic named Sulo Maki, she crisscrossed the country in her biplane, giving rides and doing aerial stunts as she traveled from town to town.

Shortly after the Peltonens moved to Bear River, a doctor discovered that Lisa's heart had been irreparably damaged by the scarlet fever she'd had as a child. She tried her best to lead a normal life, marrying at nineteen and giving birth to a daughter that same year. However, she died when she was only twenty-two. Nikko's life, too, met a tragic end back in Finland in 1939, when he was killed defending his homeland during the Russian invasion that became known as the Winter War.

# Life in America in 1905

# Historical Note

✣ ✣ ✣

Nearly a quarter of a million Finnish people left their homeland from 1900 to 1920. The reasons why so many people made the difficult decision to emigrate to other countries were many and varied; however, they generally fell into three main categories:

1. Fear of Conscription. Since Finland was a Grand Duchy of Russia, the Czar could draft Finnish citizens into the Russian army at will. Until shortly after the turn of the century, families who feared that their sons and husbands might have to join the army chose emigration as the best alternative.

2. Economic Opportunity. Though Finland relied on farming, the church along with a few wealthy landholders controlled most of the land. For many generations, family farms had been passed down to the eldest sons. This left the remaining children with no choice but to find other work. Many became poor tenant farmers known as crofters.

By 1901 seventy percent of the farms in Finland were

less than 22 acres, and many were smaller than 5 acres. The opportunity to claim 160 acres in America under the Homestead Act was a great temptation to poor Finnish farmers.

3. Religious Freedom. Finland's National Lutheran Church dominated every aspect of life. Membership in the state church was required, and everyone was expected to tithe, or give ten percent of their income. No one could marry without the permission of the church or apply for a job without a confirmation certificate. If a citizen wanted to leave the country, a certificate of character from a parish church was required to obtain a government passport.

Once they arrived in America, Finnish immigrants often joined either the Suomi Synod or the Laestadian (Apostolic) Synod of the Lutheran Church. Some became Unitarians, Methodists, and Presbyterians, while others refrained from any involvement in organized religion.

The new immigrants were mainly attracted to areas of our country that were similar in terrain to the lakes and forests of their homeland. Northern Michigan and Minnesota became the most popular places to settle. However, no matter which destination the Finns chose, they invariably found themselves on the bottom rung of the economic ladder.

Though Finland had a ninety-eight percent rate of literacy and its people were some of the best-educated in all of Europe, the Finns found English difficult to master. Since Finnish has its origin in the Finno-Ugric language family, rather than the Indo-European, Finns often became frustrated by the many differences between English and Finnish. Their poor language skills made it hard for them to compete for jobs with immigrants from the British Isles who already spoke English. The main opportunities available to the Finns involved hard physical labor. The men became lumberjacks, miners, and farm workers, while the women found employment as domestics.

The seasonal nature of the timber industry made it impossible to find consistent work, and the men who were employed in the copper mines in Michigan and the iron ore mines in Minnesota found themselves working under corrupt contract systems which demanded that they pay bribes to their foremen. Poor wages combined with unsafe working conditions, which frequently resulted in crippling injuries and deaths, made mining a risky occupation.

If the miners attempted to form unions or protest unfair working conditions, they were fired. On those occasions, such as the summer of 1907 when the miners organized a strike, the Oliver Iron Mining Company (a division of United States Steel) quickly imported hundreds of "scab" (replacement) workers to take away their jobs. The Oliver also hired "deputies" from out East who beat up workers with clubs and threw them in jail. Rather than pay the workers a fifty-cent-per-day increase, the company spent over $250,000 to break the strike.

Union members were then put on "blacklists" and banned for life from employment in the mines. Since the majority of the early union organizers were Finns, more of them were blacklisted than any other group.

To prevent further strikes, the companies also set up an industrial spy system and hired miners to file reports on their co-workers. These spies were paid to record the names of men who attended union meetings, joined Socialist organizations or clubs, or subscribed to pro-labor newspapers. Since the usual payment for this work was a dollar per day, the spies became known as "dollar a day" men. With miner's wages averaging only $2.50 per day, the temptation to join the spy system was great, and the companies often blackmailed men who were heavily in debt or had wives or children who needed medical attention.

Finns who were blacklisted had to find other means to support themselves. Farming was a logical choice, especially since so many of the immigrants had always dreamed of owning their own land. After buying hand tools and supplies to work the cutover timberlands and rock-strewn fields that were available, they began the difficult task of farming in the wilderness. Not only was the land poor for crops, but the harsh climate also allowed for a growing season of less than three frost-free months. A lifetime of back-breaking labor usually left these early homesteaders with little more than a small farm of 40 to 160 acres of land.

It is understandable then that in these early days, the Finnish rural communities stuck together. Finnish people learned to choose their companions carefully, and they rarely associated with strangers, whom they had good reason to mistrust.

The Finns started their own local cooperative stores and creameries and seed plants. Though they were regarded as "clannish" by some, the Finns gained a reputation for hard work, and their small, tightly-knit communities thrived.

In 1919 the Finnish Communists formed an alliance of cooperative stores which they successfully managed through the 1920s. In 1930 a split developed between the communist-run stores and the Central Cooperative Wholesale. That same year nineteen communist-controlled societies formed an alliance, which survived until 1940.

The Finns who did stay on as mine workers tended to get into trouble because they were outspoken advocates of unions. Despite major strikes in 1907 and 1916 and the involvement of powerful labor sympathizers from the Industrial Workers of the World (IWW), attempts at unionization failed. The mining companies effectively discouraged unions by continuing their "blacklists" and employing strong-arm tactics. In fact, the steel companies successfully blocked every attempt to organize workers until 1933, when the Congress of Industrial Organizations (CIO) finally set up Iron Range locals of the National Steel Workers Union.

An important factor in breaking the power of the steel trust was the 1928 publication of *Spies in Steel,* a book written by an investigative reporter named Frank Palmer from Denver. Palmer traveled to the Mesabi Range and exposed the Oliver Iron Mining Company's spy system by publishing names and handwriting samples of miners who had been paid to spy on their fellow workers. Though the Oliver bought and destroyed most of the copies of Palmer's book, enough of the information became public so that dozens of men left the Range in disgrace.

As the demand for iron ore production increased through World Wars I and II, Hibbing was eventually relocated two miles to the south. The original town site was taken over by United States Steel, and all the homes and buildings, which included an opera house, several theaters, a mural-filled Carnegie Library, a brand-new courthouse, and one of the most modern high schools in America, were either moved or destroyed.

Over the years, more than fifty underground mines and smaller open pit operations were gradually consolidated into one huge pit known as the Hull-Rust-Mahoning. Though the years following World War II saw a decline in natural ore production and an exodus of people from the Iron Range, in 1964, the citizens of Minnesota voted to authorize the Taconite Amendment. This legislation offered the steel companies generous tax incentives to develop the vast reserves of low grade ore. The taconite industry soon revived the local economies by building technologically advanced plants that processed lean ore into high-grade iron pellets.

Today, the Hull-Rust-Mahoning pit is the largest excavation in the world. Measuring over three miles in length, a mile across, and over five hundred feet in depth, it remains a reliable source of taconite. Present-day visitors to Hibbing can observe current mining operations from a scenic overlook on the edge of the original North Hibbing town site, and they can see firsthand this "Grand Canyon of the North," which stands as a monument to the persistence and dedication of all the immigrants who came to this land with dreams for a better life.

*While farming was common in Finland at the turn of the century, so much of the land was controlled by wealthy noblemen and the church that farm families became poorer and poorer. So, between 1900 and 1920, nearly a quarter of a million Finnish citizens set off to America where they believed farmland was abundant and accessible. Here, a typical farmhouse in Finland.*

*With the discovery of iron ore on the Mesabi Range came an influx of immigrants from more than 40 countries. They settled the land, bringing with them colorful traditions and a devotion to making better lives for their families.*

*Homes that were considered basic in Finland were far beyond their reach in America. Finnish families had to adjust to the cramped, cold, and ill-equipped housing near the mines that would become their livelihood. Their homes were so close to the mines that dynamite blasts constantly rocked the homes, and it was not unusual for rocks to crash through the roofs. Though the Finns admired the natural beauty of the forests and lakes of northeastern Minnesota, the cold and desolation were difficult hardships to overcome.*

*Built and first occupied in 1897–98, this was the Oliver Iron Mining Company General Superintendent's home in 1905. Residents of this house played key roles in the development of Hibbing. The luxury that is so evident here is an indication of just how disproportionate the distribution of wealth was at the time.*

*Early immigrants were dedicated to their children's education. To this end, the Finns supported public education. Here, classes of Finnish children pose for class photos at their schools.*

*The development of open-pit iron mining created a demand for unskilled workers. Immigrants entered the Iron Range mining areas in large numbers.*

*Rapid industrialization enabled iron ore production to grow faster than the workforce in the early twentieth century.*

*Headframes were built over underground mine shafts to support the cable and pulley systems. They lowered metal cages that delivered the miners to the various working levels, or drifts. The same cables lifted the ore to the surface in containers called skips.*

*Most of the early mining crews could not speak English, which contributed to the high accident rate. Here, two iron miners are at work in an underground drift of Sellers' Mine in Hibbing, Minnesota.*

*Conditions underground were grim. Miners had to be wary at all times of the impending dangers. Here, drift timbers are crushed by heavy, caving ground.*

*Underground carts were used to transport ore from the drift to the headframe.*

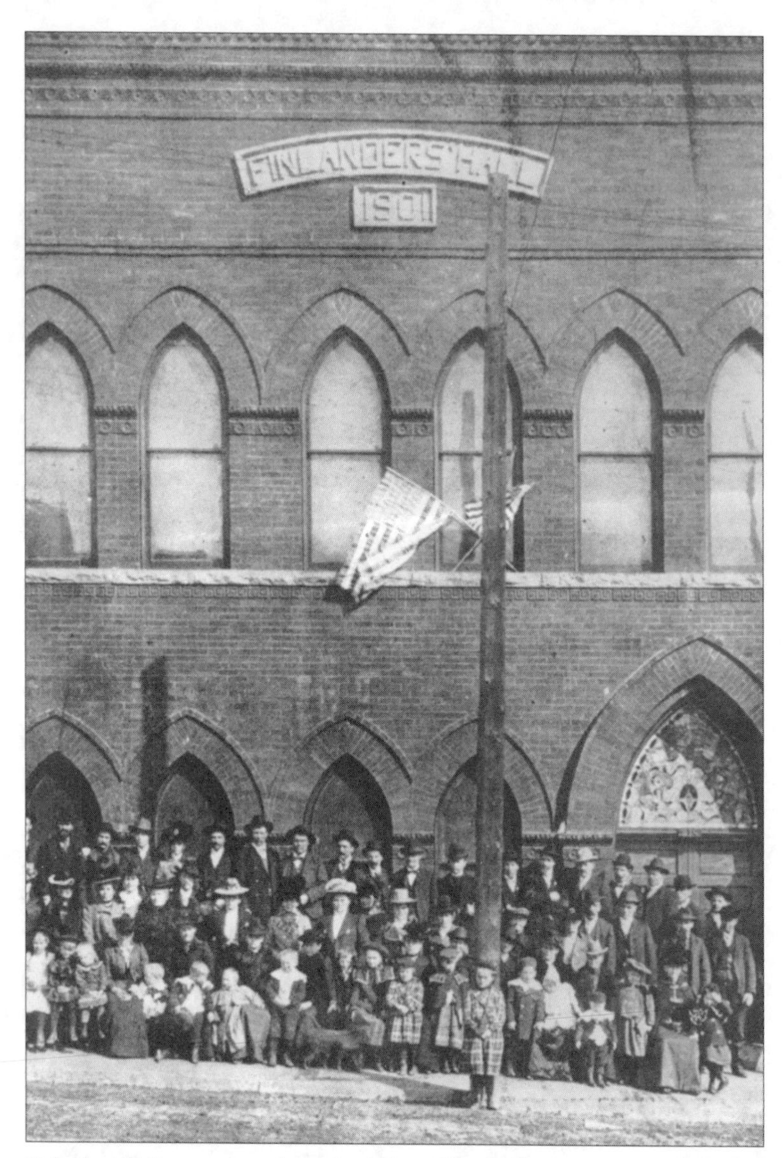


*Finlanders' Hall was a typical Socialist hall, used for both political meetings and social gatherings.*

*Since 1906, women had voted in Finland. They fought for that same right when they got to America. Here, Finnish-American women march at a suffrage parade in New York City in 1917.*

# THE MESABA ORE

and THE HIBBING NEWS.

MINNESOTA HISTORICAL SOCIETY.

The Mesaba Ore—Vol. IV—No. 11. HIBBING, MINNESOTA, SATURDAY MORNING, APRIL 15, 1905 The Hibbing News—Vol. XII—No. 14.

Clothes for the Young Fellows!

**Requiescat in Pace.**

The funeral of the late Mrs. Thomas F. Brady was held from the Catholic Church of the Blessed Sacrament at 10 o'clock Tuesday morning, and the remains were followed to the last resting place by a large cortege of sorrowing friends. Rev. Father Camache delivered a most eloquent sermon. The floral offerings were beautiful and profuse.

Mr. Brady desires The Ore to convey his feelings of thankfulness to all of those who were so kind, considerate and sympathetic during the trying ordeal which he has passed through.

**Pleasant At Home.**

Mrs. William Charles Northey gave an "at home" Wednesday afternoon for her daughter, Miss Ethel Gertrude, who on the 19th instant will become the bride of Rollin Noel Dow, of Minneapolis, and fully one hundred ladies attended. Mrs. Northey received the guests and was assisted by Mesdames Brady, LaLonde and Trenoury. Luncheon was served by Mesdames Jewett and Adams, who were assisted by Mesdames [illegible] and [illegible]. The rooms were prettily decorated with ferns, ground hemlock and daffodils. Miss Northey and Mr. Dow will be married at the home of Mr. and Mrs. Northey, No. [illegible] Mahoning street, at [illegible] o'clock in the morning, and will make their home in Minneapolis.

**Ashamed of Themselves.**

[illegible] the appearance of the members of the [illegible] Dramatic company was not such as to inspire confidence and the attendance at the Sunday night performance was in keeping with the merits of the outfit [illegible]. Fifteen people [illegible] were advertised, but eleven of them were evidently ashamed of their company and did not present themselves.

**Interests in Canada.**

A. D. Davidson and A. D. McRae returned yesterday from a business trip to Toronto and left on a late train for St. Paul. Owing to their very extensive interest in Manitoba and the Canadian territories they spend much of their time now in

## MINERS WALK OUT

### HULL-RUST MEN STRIKE AND FIFTEEN HUNDRED MINERS ARE OUT AT OLIVER MINES.

Mob Attacked Burt Mine Strippers and Two Men were Shot Dead in their Tracks — Strike Spread from Hull-Rust to all Corporation Mines in Hibbing District — Sheriff Bates and Deputies Guarding Properties — Strikers are Foreigners, Ignorant and Sullen, and Further Trouble is Feared. Labor Agitators Busy — Strikers have no Grievance — Tie up of Mesaba Range Expected to Follow — Business at a Stand-Still and the Outlook is Decidedly Serious.

Fully fifteen hundred miners in the Hibbing district are out on a strike, and there is no manner of ascertaining where the end will be. The demand is for an increase of ten cents per car for mining ore, bringing the pay up to seventy-two cents the car. Two years ago the miners of this district were receiving seventy cents a car, but the rate now paid nets the men higher wages than they were receiving in the boom year of 190[illegible], and the cost of living is less now than then. Nearly all of the miners are employed on the contract system and the average pay by the Oliver Iron Mining company, at its mines in the Hibbing district, is $2.[illegible] per day, which is the highest wage scale of any mining district in the whole Lake Superior region. The strike started without warning Tuesday morning with two hundred contract men, nearly all Austrians and Italians, going out from the Hull-Rust mine, and has since spread to all of the steel corporation mines and several independent mines and stripping operations in the Hibbing district. Aside from the original strikers, the miners and strippers say they are well satisfied with the pay they are receiving, and do not want to go out, but that they are afraid of personal violence if they continue to work; therefore the mines are all closed down, and the district is thus deprived of its daily income. Aside from the riot of Tuesday night, in which two strikers were killed, there has been no violence shown, but it is feared that more bloodshed will follow if the strikers persist in intimidating those who desire to continue working. The mines and stripping operations are being guarded by Sheriff Bates and a large force of armed deputies, and the mere appearance of these armed men has so far been sufficient to scatter the strikers as fast as they congregate. The strikers are marching in gangs from two to three hundred strong from one mine to another, where they labor with the miners and hold them from

*The* Mesaba Ore *announces: MINERS WALK OUT on April 15, 1905. The corruption of the mining industry, the unsafe conditions, and the lack of adequate compensation led to a frustrated workforce. While they tried to unite and strike to end the corruption, they were mostly ineffective. There were always people willing to fill in for the striking workers, so the mine owners and managers never felt the intended effects of the walkouts.*

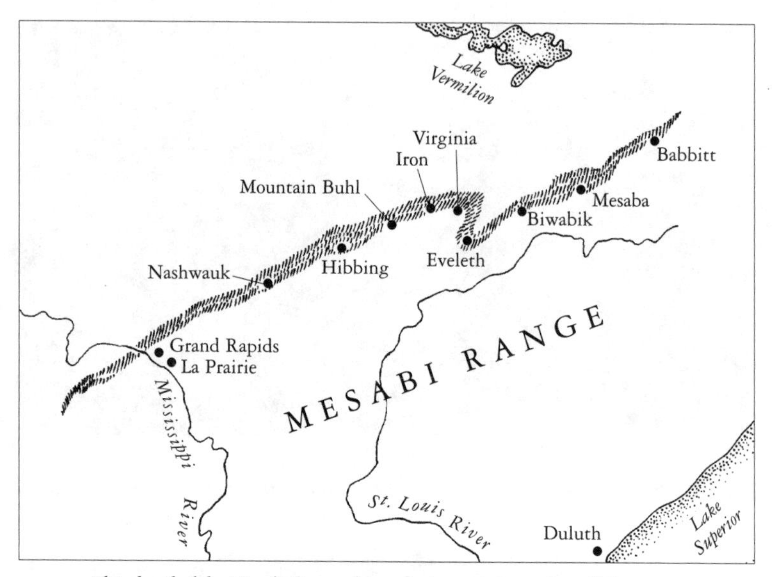


*This detail of the Mesabi Range shows the iron-mining region of Minnesota.*

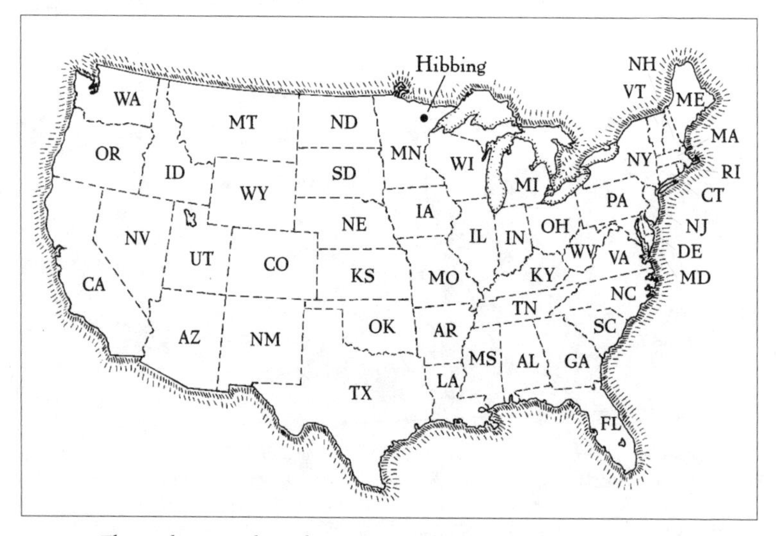


*This modern map shows the approximate location of Hibbing, Minnesota.*

# About the Author

✣ ✣ ✣

WILLIAM DURBIN is the author of three books of historical fiction, *The Broken Blade, Wintering,* and for the My Name Is America series, *The Journal of Sean Sullivan, A Transcontinental Railroad Worker. The Broken Blade* won the Great Lakes Booksellers Association Award and the Minnesota Book Award. It was named to the New York Public Library's Books for the Teen Age List and was a Bank Street College Children's Book of the Year. In a pointer review, *Kirkus Reviews* said, "Durbin's first novel is an impressive coming-of-age tale set in Montréal at the dawn of the nineteenth century . . . Readers will embrace this unusual journey and its path to true bravery, strength of character, and self-reliance."

William Durbin says, "Though I have written in a variety of genres including poetry, plays, and essays, historical fiction remains my favorite. Interviewing people and searching through period newspapers, diaries, letters, books, and magazines in an attempt to capture the character of another time is both a challenge and an adventure."

William Durbin has taught on every level from fourth grade to college. He currently teaches college composition and high-school English. Mr. Durbin has supervised writing research projects for the National Council of Teachers of English and Middlebury College's Bread Loaf School of English. He lives in Hibbing, Minnesota, with his wife, Barbara, who is also a teacher. They have a son, Reid, and a daughter, Jessica.

To Barbara, again
and always
&
To the United Steelworkers of America,
and my old local, 1938

# Acknowledgments

✣ ✣ ✣

This book would not have been possible without the support of my editor, Amy Griffin, and the production staff at Scholastic; and the dedication of my agent, Barbara Markowitz.

For help with my research I would like to thank Heikki Honkala and Annikki Ojala of Lehtimäki, Finland; Lasse Autio of the Soini Historical Society; Michael Karni, Ph.D., of Sampo Publishing; Ed Nelson, Deb Fena, and Julie Smith of the Iron Range Research Library; Halyna Myroniuk of the Immigration Research Institute in St. Paul; Lorraine Richards of Suomi College; Michelle Prigge of the Hibbing Historical Society; Tom Selinski, producer of the documentary *Spies in Steel*; John Geiselman and Marcia Smith, retired educators and former residents of old North Hibbing, and the staffs of both the Hibbing and Virginia Public Libraries.

Finally, I would like to extend my gratitude to all of my Finnish friends on the Mesabi Range who have been so willing to share stories about their heritage.

Grateful acknowledgment is made for permission to reprint the following:

✣ ✣ ✣

Cover portrait: Courtesy Lasse Autio, the Soini Historical Society, Soini, Finland.

Cover background: Photo by E. Anttila, Minnesota Historical Society, St. Paul, Minnesota.

Foldout map illustration by Bryn Barnard.

Page 156 (top): Farmhouse in Finland, photo from Anniki Ojala, Lehtimaki.

Page 156 (bottom): Hibbing Houses, Aubin Photo Service, Hibbing, Minnesota.

Page 157: School house, Methodist Church, and shacks at Hibbing, Minnesota on December 21, 1900, from the collections of the Minnesota Historical Society.

Page 158: Oliver Iron Mining Company Superintendent's home — 1905. Photo courtesy of the John Chisholm family. *A Photo Essay of an Iron Mining Community, Hibbing Minnesota,* by Lorraine DeMillo.

Page 159 (top): Finnish-American School, Esko, Minnesota, 1904. Walfrid J. Jokinen, University of Minnesota, Immigration History Research Center.

Page 159 (bottom): Finnish Log School in East Eveleth, Minnesota, April 1915. University of Minnesota, Immigration History Research Center.

Page 160 (top): Miners on steps. University of Minnesota, Immigration History Research Center.

Page 160 (bottom): open pit mine, Iron Range Research Center, Chisholm, Minnesota.

Page 161: Headframe. Aubin Photo Service, Hibbing, Minnesota.

Page 162: Two Miners underground. Underwood and Underwood, Minnesota Historical Society.

Page 163 (top): Crushing of Drift. Iron Range Research Center, Chisholm, Minnesota.

Page 163 (bottom): Underground, cart carrying ore, Iron Range Research Center, Chisholm, Minnesota.

Page 164: Finlanders' Hall. Amerikan Albumi, University of Minnesota, Immigration History Research Center.

Page 165 (top): Finnish-American women "standard bearers" marching in women's suffrage parade, New York, 1917. University of Minnesota, Immigration History Research Center.

Page 165 (bottom): *Mesaba Ore.* Iron Range Research Center, Chisholm, Minnesota.

Page 166: Maps by Heather Saunders.

## Other books in the My Name Is America series

*The Journal of William Thomas Emerson*
*A Revolutionary War Patriot*
by Barry Denenberg

*The Journal of James Edmond Pease*
*A Civil War Union Soldier*
by Jim Murphy

*The Journal of Joshua Loper*
*A Black Cowboy*
by Walter Dean Myers

*The Journal of Scott Pendleton Collins*
*A World War II Soldier*
by Walter Dean Myers

*The Journal of Sean Sullivan*
*A Transcontinental Railroad Worker*
by William Durbin

*The Journal of Ben Uchida*
*Citizen 13559, Mirror Lake Internment Camp*
by Barry Denenberg

*The Journal of Jasper Jonathan Pierce*
*A Pilgrim Boy*
by Ann Rinaldi

*The Journal of Wong Ming-Chung*
*A Chinese Miner*
by Laurence Yep

*The Journal of Augustus Pelletier*
*The Lewis & Clark Expedition*
by Kathryn Lasky

**While the events described and some of the characters in this book may be based on actual historical events and real people, Otto Peltonen is a fictional character, created by the author, and his journal and its epilogue are works of fiction.**



✣ ✣ ✣



---

Library of Congress Cataloging-in-Publication Data
Durbin, William, 1951–
The Journal of Otto Peltonen, a Finnish Immigrant / by William Durbin.
—1st ed.
p. cm. — (My Name is America)
Summary: In 1905, fifteen-year-old Otto describes in his journal how he travels from Finland to America, joining his father in a dreary iron mining community in Minnesota and becoming involved in a union fight for better working conditions.

ISBN 0-439-09254-X

[1. Emigration and immigration — Fiction. 2. Finnish-Americans — Fiction. 3. Iron mines and mining — Fiction. 4. Strikes and lockouts — Fiction. 5. Minnesota — Fiction. 6. Diaries — Fiction.] I. Title. II. Series.

PZ7.D9323 Jm 2000
[Fic]—dc21 00-021919
CIP

---

10 9 8 7 6 5 4 3 2 1 0/0 01 02 03 04

The display type was set in Locarno Light Semibold.
The text type was set in Berling Roman.
Book design by Elizabeth B. Parisi
Photo research by Zoe Moffitt

Printed in the U.S.A. 23
First edition, September 2000

✣ ✣ ✣